Readers love

A Heart Without Borders

by ANDREW GREY

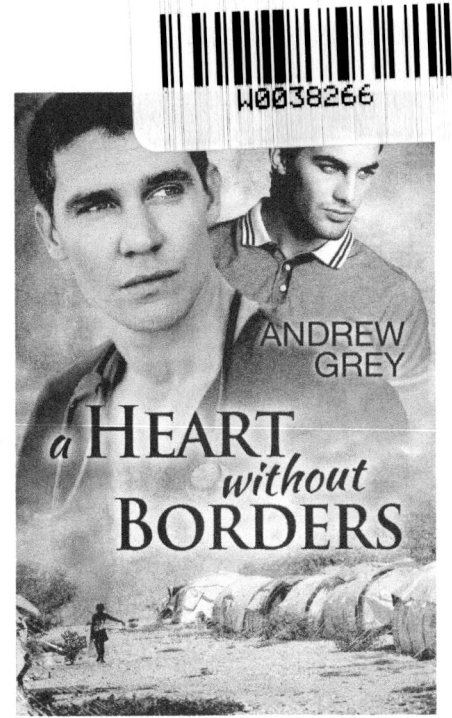

"Andrew Grey flexes his writing muscles… There is no doubt in my mind that this book will stay with me for a long time."
—The Novel Approach

"In true Andrew Grey fashion, this book delivers not only a romance but a powerful lesson on the courage, hope and optimism of people in a country devastated by disaster and poverty."
—Hearts on Fire

"The characters were exceptionally well written and the plot was interesting to say the least."
—Top 2 Bottom Reviews

"The author does an outstanding job in describing Haiti as I have no doubt it is today… Highly recommended."
—On Top Down Under Reviews

"Grey has delivered another masterpiece with the story of Wes, Anthony, and René. You will seriously be on the edge of your seat throughout…"
—MM Good Book Reviews

Published by DREAMSPINNER PRESS
http://www.dreamspinnerpress.com

By ANDREW GREY (continued)

CHEMISTRY
Organic Chemistry • Biochemistry • Electrochemistry

GOOD FIGHT
The Good Fight • The Fight Within • The Fight for Identity • Takoda and Horse

LOVE MEANS…
Love Means… No Shame • Love Means… Courage
Love Means… No Boundaries
Love Means… Freedom • Love Means … No Fear
Love Means… Healing
Love Means… Family • Love Means… Renewal • Love Means… No Limits
Love Means… Patience • Love Means… Endurance

SENSES
Love Comes Silently • Love Comes in Darkness
Love Comes Home • Love Comes Around

SEVEN DAYS
Seven Days • Unconditional Love

STORIES FROM THE RANGE
A Shared Range • A Troubled Range • An Unsettled Range
A Foreign Range • An Isolated Range • A Volatile Range • A Chaotic Range

TALES FROM KANSAS
Dumped in Oz • Stuck in Oz • Trapped in Oz

TASTE OF LOVE
A Taste of Love • A Serving of Love • A Helping of Love
A Slice of Love

WITHOUT BORDERS
A Heart Without Borders • A Spirit Without Borders

WORK OUT
Spot Me • Pump Me Up • Core Training • Crunch Time
Positive Resistance • Personal Training • Cardio Conditioning
Work Me Out (Anthology)

Published by DREAMSPINNER PRESS
http://www.dreamspinnerpress.com

a SPIRIT *without* BORDERS

ANDREW GREY

Published by
DREAMSPINNER PRESS

5032 Capital Circle SW, Suite 2, PMB# 279, Tallahassee, FL 32305-7886 USA
http://www.dreamspinnerpress.com/

A Spirit Without Borders
© 2015 Andrew Grey.

Cover Art
© 2015 L.C. Chase.
http://www.lcchase.com
Cover content is for illustrative purposes only and any person depicted on the cover is a model.

ISBN: 978-1-63476-227-4
Digital ISBN: 978-1-63476-228-1
Library of Congress Control Number: 2015905842
First Edition July 2015

Printed in the United States of America

This paper meets the requirements of
ANSI/NISO Z39.48-1992 (Permanence of Paper).

To all the doctors and health workers who put themselves in harm's way in order to ease the suffering of the sick all over the world.

Chapter 1

"HELLO," DILLON McDowell said as he walked into the hospital room, noticing that the quarantine sign was gone, as was the cart with gloves, aprons, and breathing masks. "How are you feeling?"

"Okay," Mikey Thorson said tiredly, but his eyes were clear and his skin was dry. That was a huge improvement over the past few days. "Am I gonna die?"

"No," Dillon answered with a smile and gently sat on the edge of Mikey's bed. This was the third time he'd asked the same question, and the first time, Dillon had swallowed hard. He'd answered the same way then, but truthfully he hadn't really known. Mikey had been fading fast and losing energy by the second. Dillon knew he needed to reassure Mikey somehow, and even though the nurse had looked at him over his exhausted, tiny frame, Dillon had not been ready to give up, and it seemed neither had Mikey. "You're going to be fine now." When Mikey pulled his hand from under the blanket and held it up, Dillon did the same thing. "Scouts' honor. You're going to get better now, and soon you'll be able to go home."

"Are Mommy and Daddy here?"

"You were sleeping so they went to get something to eat. They'll be back in just a few minutes."

Mikey smiled, and that was so good to see. "I'm hungry," Mikey said softly, which was another really good sign.

"I'll talk to the nurse and we'll get something yummy in here for you." Dillon would place one of his special orders that the kitchen hated but that always made his younger patients really happy. The hospital was top-notch, but the food left something to be desired. Dillon wasn't above cutting through everything and everyone to get what his patients needed. "What do you like to eat?"

"Ice cream, strawberries, chocolate," Mikey answered.

"How about something without sugar," Dillon said, keeping his voice as soothing as possible.

"Chicken nuggets."

Of course, a kid staple. "Macaroni and cheese?"

"Yeah."

"Okay. I'll see what I can do." Dillon stood up.

"Don't leave me alone," Mikey said, and Dillon nodded. He had other rounds to do, but he wouldn't go anywhere.

"Do you like baseball?" Dillon asked. He zeroed in on the family picture someone had placed beside the bed showing Mikey in his baseball uniform.

"Yeah. I'm a real good hitter. I can't catch so well, though. Daddy says he's going to help me. Maybe when I get out and go home, Daddy can play catch with me."

"That sounds like a lot of fun." Dillon kept the emotion out of his voice. Dillon's own father had never played catch with him. It hadn't mattered how many times Dillon had asked—his father had always been too busy. Eventually he stopped asking to do things with him or for his dad to come to his games. His father never had time for that either. Sometimes Dillon had wondered why his parents had even had children if all they did was ignore them.

The door to the room opened and Mikey's mother and father came in slowly, all smiles. They had worried for a week about their son, spending day and night at the hospital. Dillon stood up and smiled at Mikey. "I'll stop by and see you later," Dillon said, and after sharing a smile with Mikey's parents, he left the room and headed for the nurses' station. There he updated Mikey's chart, then left the area after briefly greeting the nurses on duty.

Dillon made the rest of his rounds before going to his small office in the hospital, where he checked his messages and found one asking him to see Milton, the hospital administrator, at his earliest convenience. Dillon was about to leave again when Carlton Grant walked into his office and closed the door.

"Do you have to be a total ass?" Carlton asked, eyes blazing, voice dripping with indignation. "I brought you in to consult on the Thorson case, not take it over."

Dillon crossed his arms over his chest. "You had no idea what was going on and were treating him for the flu. He didn't have the flu. He had measles."

"There were no spots," Carlton said.

"Sometimes, in rare cases, measles don't manifest that way, at least not to start with. You should have checked his history. I knew what he had from the other symptoms, and I spoke to Mikey's parents about his health history. They don't believe in immunizations." Dillon had his own opinions about that, and it seemed Mikey's parents had changed their minds as well after nearly losing their son to a disease that could easily be prevented. They had reportedly already made an appointment at the hospital to have Mikey immunized against other infectious diseases in a month, once he was fully recovered. "That led me to the diagnosis, and his parents requested that he be put under my care."

"You still didn't need to be such a jerk about it and tell everyone," Carlton said.

"That boy could have died, and you're worried about your ego," Dillon said. "Get over it and concentrate on your patients."

"Ego...." Carlton sputtered. "God, I'm surprised there's space for you or me in this room with your ego. Everyone makes mistakes, and I called you in because I needed your help. It's what we do when we have a case that isn't progressing. We ask for help. I did, and you made me a laughingstock because of it." Carlton turned toward the door.

"No, I didn't," Dillon said. "I helped the patient recover, that's all. There was no campaign to ruin your reputation, and I didn't go around talking about you behind your back. I did my job and I did it well." Dillon couldn't for the life of him understand where this venom was coming from. "Mikey is recovering and he's going to go home in a day or so, once he gets his strength back."

Carlton yanked the door open and stormed out into the hallway. Dillon shrugged and gave him no more thought before leaving his office and heading up to Administration in the older section of the hospital complex. He approached Milton's office, opened the door, and stepped into the outer reception area. Clare sat at her desk, typing away like a madwoman. She could be the quintessential secretary in a sitcom. She was gorgeous from head to toe and turned heads wherever she went. A lot of the staff thought she had been hired for her looks, but that was so not the case. Dillon knew Clare was sharp as a tack and rarely missed anything.

"He's been waiting to see you." Clare knew most of what crossed Milton's desk, but she never gave anything away. "Go right on in."

Dillon walked to Milton's door and opened it. Like many hospital administrators, Milton was a master at making too few resources cover all the things that the hospital needed, so his office was spartan, just like the man.

"Please have a seat," Milton said after they shook hands. "I have an opportunity for you." He motioned to a chair and Dillon sat down.

"All right," Dillon said warily. He had been around long enough to know that when administration said "opportunity," it generally meant something not so pleasant. Like, "You have the *opportunity* to work in the morgue."

"Last year you had expressed an interest in an assignment in Haiti with Doctors Without Borders, but things just weren't in place for us to let you go for six months. Well, they've come calling, and I've made some arrangements. They're in dire need of doctors with infectious disease experience, and since that is most definitely your area, I put your name forward."

"So what changed between this year and last?" Dillon asked. There hadn't been any new hires in his area in the last year.

"Quite frankly, the staff needs a break from you." Milton leaned forward in his chair. "Don't get me wrong—you're an amazing physician, and if my child were to get sick, I'd want you on her case, but the other doctors don't like to work with you."

"I do my job."

"You do it well. Sometimes, though I hate to say it, too well. There isn't a case that you haven't been able to take on and make progress with." Milton held up his hand, and Dillon closed his mouth. "I'm not saying there aren't disappointments. That happens in medicine. We lose patients—it's part of the job."

"I don't understand what you're trying to say. I'm too good at my job? That isn't possible."

"Of course not. But you rub the other staff the wrong way. Yes, you're good at your job and you know it. There isn't a microbe or virus that doesn't live in fear of you. The thing is that you know it."

"Is this about Carlton?"

"No. You saving that boy was brilliant, and this has nothing to do with him. I've spoken to your supervisor, and we both feel that you need to be challenged and maybe to learn a little humility. So when this opportunity came up, we thought you might have a chance at both."

"So where are you sending me?"

"I'm not sending you anywhere. This choice is up to you. Doctors Without Borders doesn't want anyone who isn't prepared for what they are going to face. The government is setting up a number of clinics in Liberia to help contain the Ebola outbreak there, and infectious disease specialists are desperately needed. Right now there is limited effectiveness in treating Ebola. Everyone is hoping that if enough brilliant minds focus on the task, more treatments and effective drugs can be developed. The opportunity we have for you is to go to Liberia and work in one of these Ebola hospitals. They need your expertise, and you need the challenge."

Dillon humphed. "So you want to get rid of me." He shifted nervously in his chair. He knew he was a damned good doctor and one of the best at what he did. What was so wrong with acting like it? He'd worked hard for years to become the doctor he was. Why in the hell should he have to hide it?

Milton had relaxed, but he once again leaned closer. "Everyone you work with is a good doctor or we wouldn't have them on staff. But many complain that they feel put down after they work with you."

"What do you want me to do? Screw up just to keep them happy?"

"No. We want you to grow as a doctor and as a person. Let me ask you this: If I had said nothing to you about the feelings of the other doctors, would we be having this conversation? Or would you be making appointments to get all the shots you needed before going home to pack for Liberia."

Dillon had to admit that Milton was right. "I'll give you that," he reluctantly admitted. "I'm here to do a job and to save patients' lives. That's why I became a doctor."

"I know. It's why every one of those people out there became doctors as well. Remember that. Each and every person on staff has the same goal, and we all need to work together for that to happen. You need to become part of a team, and you won't be able to be successful in Liberia if you try to go it alone all the time. There are too many challenges for any one person. So do you think you're up to it?"

"Hell yes, I'm up to it," Dillon answered quickly.

"Okay, then." Milton pulled open a drawer and got out a file. "Normally these assignments are six months, but because of the environment, the Centers for Disease Control is only recommending three months for these assignments. You'll leave in four weeks. I know you've gotten a lot of the immunizations you'll need, but make sure you're protected as much as possible before you leave. Of course your job here will be waiting for you when you return." Milton stood, and Dillon did as well. "I want to stress that we want you here and are happy you're on staff. You save lives and do one hell of a job, and I know you'll do a great job over there as well." They shook hands again, and then Dillon left Milton and went back to his office.

DILLON HAD to concentrate for the rest of the day, and once he'd seen all his patients, he stopped into Mikey's room to check on how he was. "Hi, Dr. Dillon," Mikey said with a grin as he sat up in bed, eating from a plate of macaroni and cheese and chicken nuggets. "This is good."

"I'm glad, buddy." He'd gotten the kitchen to make it special for him, and he'd even told them to make sure they got good nuggets and the mac and cheese from the blue box, not the stuff they usually served that tasted like nothing. Yeah, he probably wasn't popular, but Mikey's smile was all he needed at the moment.

"We're so grateful to you," Nelson Thorson said, towering over Dillon when he stood. The man was intimidatingly tall, but his smile was warm and genuine.

"I'm glad I could help."

"We have appointments with our doctor for next week, and Mikey is going to be getting all the shots he needs."

Mikey groaned and put down his fork. "More pokes." He rubbed his arm, and Dillon stifled a laugh.

"I hate them too," Dillon said in a whisper. "As a kid, when they gave me a shot, I used to kick the nurse. But think about it this way. If you have the shots, then you'll be less likely to be in the hospital again and you won't have to eat the yucky mac and cheese they usually serve." Dillon shuddered, and Mikey laughed and returned to his dinner.

"It's good to see him eating like that," Mikey's mother, Ramona, said as she fussed around Mikey.

"We're all happy about it." Dillon turned to Mikey. "You gave us quite a scare, but you and your dad will be out playing catch in no time." Dillon smiled at the now happy family and left the room, returning Mikey's wave as he saw him go back to his dinner.

Dillon went back to his office, got his things, and got ready to leave. He'd just pulled out of the parking lot when his phone buzzed in his pocket. The ring then sounded in his car, so he pressed the Bluetooth button to answer it on the steering wheel. "Hello."

"Dillon." His mother's voice came through the speakers like a buzz saw. "You do remember that you're expected for dinner this evening, right? Your father is entertaining some business associates, and his client is bringing his daughter so you can meet her."

He groaned silently as he got on the freeway heading out of Milwaukee and toward the northern suburbs. All he wanted was to go home, and he hated the thought of another of his mother's stuffy and dull dinner parties to entertain one of his father's many business associates, who all seemed to have daughters interested in marrying a doctor. "I'm tired and I've had a long day at the hospital."

"Don't give me that old excuse. You promised you'd come, and your father made a commitment based on that, so go home and clean up. It's black tie, so please dress appropriately." She hung up, and Dillon groaned. He checked the time, then pressed the accelerator to get home more quickly. Ten minutes later, after swearing a few times and getting off the freeway an exit earlier than he intended, he drove into the quiet bedroom community of Whitefish Bay and turned into the alley behind his house, pulling his BMW into the garage.

Dillon got out and walked through his backyard, wishing he had the time to work out here and get all the weeds pulled. He needed to hire someone to clean it up, but he kept forgetting. Of course his mother would probably send her gardener over if he asked, but he was damned well not going to do that. His mother was demanding enough—he wasn't going to let her think he wasn't capable of taking care of his home. Otherwise she'd insist he move back to the family home, and he'd worked hard to get out of that pile of stone.

He went inside, dropped his case on the granite tabletop in the newly remodeled kitchen, and hurried up the stairs. He undressed in his bedroom and went right to the bathroom to shower. When he'd seen the house a year earlier, he'd fallen in love with the place. It wasn't huge, but the exterior was stone and the inside relatively plain. It had been built very solidly in the thirties and it was comfortable, with a working fireplace and hardwood floors. The ceilings in the upper floor slanted in places with the roof line, but he thought it made the house seem comfortable and cozy. Best of all it was his—the first place he'd ever had that was only his, and he absolutely loved it. His mother, of course, hated it.

He showered quickly, but took more time to dress. He checked himself in the mirror and admired how he looked in his Armani tuxedo for about two seconds, then turned off the lights and descended the stairs so fast he almost tripped. He grabbed his wallet and keys before leaving the house once again and driving east toward Lake Drive. It took him ten minutes to pull up to the imposing classic stone mansion that his parents called home. He drove through the open gate, past the fountain, and along the manicured lawn before parking off to the side and walking to the door as slowly as possible. He didn't want to be here, but ignoring an invitation from his mother was not worth the fight.

He opened the door and walked right inside, the sound of cocktail conversation wafting from the formal living room just off the hall. His mother smiled when he walked in, and Dillon saw her look him over before standing up, a black cocktail dress hugging the curves she worked hard to maintain. He leaned close and kissed her on the cheek and then shook hands with his father.

"You remember Claude and Marlene Grovner," his father said.

"Of course," Dillon lied, shaking hands with both of them. He'd probably met them, but he didn't remember at all.

"Their daughter, Camille," his father continued. Dillon shook her hand as well, and he was relieved when she didn't giggle and blush. The last time his parents had designs to marry him off to the daughter of one of his father's business contacts, the daughter had done exactly that.

"It's nice to meet you," Dillon said formally and took a seat away from her. He did his best not to shake his head or pound the arm of the chair in frustration. He hated situations like this. He had told his parents he was gay while he was still in medical school. He'd done it in this very room, and they had looked at each other and then back at him.

"That's nice, dear," his mother had said in her placating way and refused to hear any more about it. Until he'd moved out, Dillon had lived in their self-centered world, where money and status ruled and denial was a weapon wielded to keep anything that interfered with their image of themselves at bay.

His father poured him a martini, and Dillon took the glass and slowly sipped the drink. He didn't really like them, but it was the convention.

"How are things at the hospital?" Claude asked him.

"Very well."

"I understand you're building quite a name for yourself with your diagnostic skills," Claude added with a slight smile.

"Yes, I seem to be. Doctors Without Borders has requested my help overseas, so I consider that quite an honor." Dillon took another sip of his drink and watched his parents' faces as they shared one of those looks that said there was going to be plenty of discussion later, at least on their parts.

"Where do they want you to go?" Camille asked in her pleasant voice.

"Liberia," Dillon answered.

His mother coughed slightly and set down her glass. His father actually spilled a little of his drink in his rush to set the glass down.

"The World Health Organization is setting up a number of clinics to try to contain the Ebola outbreak there, and they want me to help at one of them. It's a huge honor, and in my specialty, it's the opportunity of a lifetime." The fact that it made his parents uncomfortable was both a side benefit and an indication that they cared for him—the latter being rare as hen's teeth. "I need to schedule the few immunizations I'm going to require, and then I'll leave in a month."

"Why can't you stay here? How can you be sure you won't get that awful disease?" his mother said and then gulped from her glass. "We do worry about you."

"I know, Mother," he answered as gently as he could.

"How long will you be gone?" Marlene asked. "That seems so exciting. I know it can be dangerous, I suppose, but it has to be pretty amazing to be on the forefront of your profession." She glanced at her daughter, and Dillon stifled a groan. He always felt like some prize thoroughbred whenever his parents did this, and he figured it was time for them to stop.

"It is, and the timing is good. The hospital offered me leave to go, and I don't have a boyfriend at the moment, so there are no personal entanglements to prevent me from going. And it's only for three months. Then I'll be able to return to my job at the hospital." Dillon knew he'd rambled a little, but he also saw that they got the boyfriend reference he'd thrown in. Hopefully that would put an end to the matchmaking activities for the evening. "When is dinner, Mother?"

"A few minutes," she answered absently. Dillon wasn't sure what she was thinking. Sometimes his mother was predictable enough that he could guess, but not at the moment. His father downed his drink and made another. Mr. and Mrs. Grovner seemed completely unfazed, and Camille sat back in her chair with a smile. When dinner was announced, Dillon stood and offered his arm to Camille, who took it and seemed to move very slowly.

"Thank you," she whispered as they moved toward the dining room at a glacial place. "My parents think that they need to find me a husband, and it drives me crazy. I have a girlfriend at the moment and these... things always hurt her because she knows what my folks are doing." Dillon smiled, liking her more by the second. "They think it's a rebellious phase that I'm going through."

"Stick to your guns," Dillon said with a smile. "Maybe when I get back, we can have dinner. I'd like to meet your girlfriend." He made sure no one heard, and after ushering Camille to her place, he took his next to her.

The food was amazing and the surroundings opulent, with low lighting dancing off the crystal on the table from the chandelier hanging above. Dillon's father and Claude talked business while his mother and Marlene talked decorators and gardeners. Thankfully, Camille was bright and lively, so they conversed in low tones through much of the meal and dessert. For coffee, they moved back to the living room under the guise of getting comfortable, but then it was obvious that no one was. The chairs were way too stiff, and his parents were wound tight as drums.

Finally, the evening ended with Claude and Marlene standing to say good-bye. Camille did the same, and Dillon walked her to the door. They all said good night, and Dillon then turned to go back inside.

As soon as the front door closed, the claws came out. "How dare you say something like that in front of our friends," his mother spat.

"What?" Dillon was determined to make her say it.

"That *boyfriend* business."

"Please. I told you years ago that I'm gay. This is my life, not some Victorian melodrama, and I don't appreciate you trying to fix me up like this. Neither does Camille." That would turn the knife a little.

"And what's this about Liberia? People are dying there, and even here. Do you think I want some son of mine over there to—?"

"What—help?" Dillon countered. "Look, I've made up my mind, and I don't need or require your permission. I also don't need your help to find a wife. I'm not going to marry a woman and that's final."

"Who is going to carry on the family name and business? I know you aren't interested, but I hoped you'd give me grandchildren." His father seemed unusually disappointed.

"I don't know what my life is going to be like yet. But I do know there is a snowball's chance in hell that I'm going to marry a woman, so please stop this. You only end up disappointed, and I have to explain things to yet another girl." His mother gasped slightly. "Of course I tell them, Mother. I have ethics and I don't want them hurt." Dillon checked his watch. "I need to go. I have to be at the hospital early in the morning." He kissed his mother good-bye and then hugged his father, who didn't seem to know how to react. "You don't need to worry about me. I have my own life." He wanted to add that maybe they needed to figure out one of their own, but he kept quiet.

He opened the front door and headed out into the night. The air was crisp and refreshing, with the breeze off the lake carrying the scent of the water. He did love it here and thought about walking around the house to the bluff, but got in his car instead. After an evening with his parents, Liberia was starting to look pretty good. He'd traveled after college, but this would be an adventure that could change his life.

Chapter 2

DILLON WAS not prepared. As much as he read and tried to be ready for his trip, he was not at all prepared for the chaos and the smell as thousands of people milled and herded their way through the stiflingly hot airport in Monrovia, the Liberian capital. He wanted nothing more than to get out of this building, but the lines moved at a snail's pace, and Dillon gasped for breath and any sort of refreshing breeze. Even the ceiling fans didn't seem to do a dang thing. By the time he got to the front of the line and had his documents stamped, he was soaked with sweat.

Finally Dillon retrieved his luggage and headed toward the exit with throngs of others. He had papers in hand with his instructions and looked around the airport's arrivals area. Finally a man rushed up to him. "Dillon McDowell?" he said rather haltingly.

"Yes," Dillon said and moved closer.

"I am Uriel. I am your ride." He offered a huge smile. "Come with me." Uriel turned, and Dillon followed, weaving through hordes of people carrying bags and baskets, dressed in every color known to man. The noise was nearly deafening. Somehow he managed to keep up as they went outside. The air was even hotter, but, thank God, there was a breeze. He inhaled and did his best not to cough. He had truly not been prepared for any of this, and he reminded himself that he was on an adventure.

"I take you to hotel for tonight. Tomorrow we go to hospital. Okay?"

"That would be great." Dillon was tired and desperately needed to clean up. He followed Uriel to an old car and stowed his luggage in the trunk, which was held together with gray tape. He got in next to Uriel and waited for him to start the engine. As soon as Uriel did, cool air blew from the vents. There was a God after all. Dillon held up his arms and let the air flow over him. He sighed and closed his eyes.

"We go now," Uriel said and started the car moving forward into chaotic traffic. There were signs, but no one seemed to obey them. Dillon held on and hoped like hell they'd make it to the hotel in one piece. It took about an hour, but eventually they pulled up in front of a building that looked surprisingly modern. It wasn't palatial, by any means, but it seemed nice enough. Dillon got out and pulled his luggage from the trunk as Uriel walked around to where he stood. "I get you tomorrow morning at nine. No be late."

"Where are you staying?" Dillon asked, and Uriel pointed across the road to what looked like a building about ready to fall down. It took him a second to realize Uriel wasn't pointing to the building but indicating a general direction.

"I go home, see my family."

"Okay. Thank you for the ride, and I'll see you in the morning." Dillon picked up his bags and walked into the hotel. It was cooler than outside, but still warm. He supposed the heat was something he would have to get used to. He approached the staff members at the front desk and told them his name. Thankfully, they were indeed expecting him, and after he checked in, Dillon was given an old-fashioned key and pointed toward the stairs. The lift was out of order, the desk clerk explained.

Not that it mattered. Dillon carried his bags up the stairs to the third floor. He found his room and let himself in. The room was stifling, but there was air-conditioning of a sort. He turned it on and prayed that it worked. It did, so Dillon put his bags aside and flopped down on the bed. He was bone weary, and once the room cooled, he fell asleep without getting undressed.

When he woke, he was starved. He went downstairs and found the hotel restaurant. He had little idea what was on offer and guessed as best he could, placing his order after puzzling through the dishes, making sure to order bottled water and staying away from raw fruit and vegetables. What he got smelled wonderful and looked amazing. It was spicy and full of flavor. He ate it as hot as he could stand and enjoyed it without asking too many questions. Then he went back to his room—now that his stomach was full, he was tired again. He got undressed, cleaned up, keeping his nose, eyes, and mouth out of the water stream, and climbed into bed, making sure he set an alarm so he wouldn't be late. Time seemed meaningless. His body had no idea where he was, so he simply slept.

THE FOLLOWING morning, he packed, checked out, and found Uriel waiting for him. His bags were once again placed in the trunk and he got in the car. "How long is the drive?"

"In distance not so much, but it take a few hours," Uriel said, and Dillon got in and settled for a long drive.

The scenery was amazing, especially once Monrovia faded in the distance. The land was green with occasional grass-roofed buildings passing by. The farther they got from the city, the rougher the roads became, and soon they had slowed to a crawl. He now understood what Uriel meant. They weren't going all that far in distance, but there were points when they could have walked faster. Eventually, after Dillon felt completely shaken and stirred, they pulled into a compound with sturdier-looking buildings, one of which had a red cross on the roof. "Thank you," Dillon said, "I appreciate all your help," as his bags were unloaded.

Uriel smiled, and Dillon wondered what he was supposed to do. Uriel shook his hand, flashed another smile, and then hurried back toward the car. Dillon watched him go and then picked up his bags and walked toward the hospital, hoping someone would be able to explain where he was to go.

He walked to the entrance, where he expected another scene of chaos, sort of like a war zone, but instead it was quiet.

"Can I help you?" a woman with huge eyes and dark skin asked in perfect English.

"Yes, I'm Dr. Dillon McDowell. I'm starting work here." Dillon tried to keep the nervous excitement out of his voice.

"The doctors' area is just down there. They should be able to help you." She hurried off, and Dillon stared after her for a second before following her instructions. Dillon knocked on a door down the short hallway.

"Hi. You look a little lost." a man with the deepest eyes Dillon had ever seen asked when he opened the door.

"Dr. Dillon McDowell," he said, and the man opened the door further. "I hope I'm expected."

"And needed. Please come in." He stepped back. "I'm Will Scarlet and no, you don't get to make any Robin Hood jokes." He smiled. "This is Joseph Granger. There are others, but they're on duty at the moment. I'm sure you'll meet them soon. How was your trip?" Will looked down at his bags. "I see you've literally come right in. No worries. We'll get you settled."

Joseph stood, shook Dillon's hand, and then headed to the door. "I need to get busy, but I'm sure I'll see you later." He left the room and closed the door behind him.

"Is it always like that?"

"Yes." Will chuckled slightly. "Everyone around here works hard and very long hours. We have five doctors here, and about a hundred or more patients at any given time, sometimes more when the virus spreads quickly." He lifted one of Dillon's bags. "Come on. I'll show you your quarters, and then we can go over protocols and duty schedules."

"Are you in charge?"

"Not really, but we all help out as best we can. Dr. Patel— Sanjay—is out in the field. We work with nearby populations to try to educate them about Ebola, how it spreads, and what they can do to detect it early and help prevent contracting the disease. It's an uphill battle, because there has been so much fear associated with the disease and so much misinformation generated within the local populations."

"Is that what most of our patients have?"

"Yes. We are a facility that specializes in the treatment of Ebola. We handle other diseases as well, but in this area it's Ebola that keeps us on our toes. I assume you're familiar with it?"

"Yes," Dillon answered dryly. "I specialize in infectious diseases, so I've read every paper and protocol that's been published."

Will set down his bag as they approached one of the hospital doors. "That may serve you well in the States, but it isn't likely to be much help here. Yes, we know how Ebola spreads and how to protect ourselves from contracting it. But this disease seems to defy all of the rules that your papers and protocols describe. Here it's down and dirty medicine, quite literally. People come in with sky-high fevers, weakened already by malnutrition, and they stand little chance." Will picked up his bag once again. "It's no cake walk. Back in the States, there are organizations to help, quarantines, antibiotics, antivirals, IVs, plenty of clean water and nutrition. Many of the people we see have parasites even before they contract Ebola, so we're fighting a large number of issues at the same time."

"A little defensive?" Dillon chided as lightly as he could, raising his eyebrow when Will turned toward him. Dillon swallowed hard. This was definitely not going to be anything like what he imagined.

"Every new doctor who comes in here thinks they're going to change the world, and most of them get chewed up and spat out." Will pushed open the door, and they stepped out into the sweltering heat. "The doctors' quarters are over there in the shade of those trees. You'll come to adore that shade. We have electricity, but there isn't enough for any sort of air-conditioning. That's why the roofs are highly peaked—the heat can rise and we have a chance at not sweltering to death."

"Thanks for the warning."

"I saw your bio and I know you come from where it's cold. Me, I'm from Florida. Heat is no problem for me." Will walked across the yard and pushed open one of the doors. "You'll be sharing with me."

Dillon wasn't sure how he felt about that. He'd spent the past ten minutes trying not to admire the way Will's pants hugged his hips just so or the way his shirt clung tightly to his back, giving a hint of what was below. He was here to do a job, and he needed to get his mind off handsome Will and on the task at hand.

Will stepped inside, and Dillon followed. It was dark. The window was covered, most likely to keep out the sun and heat. But it was surprisingly comfortable inside. Will placed his suitcase near the foot of the one bed and then sat on the other.

"Not much privacy, is there?"

"Not here. That's something we really don't have the time or space for. I'm sure you'll get used to it. We all had to at one point or another."

"How long have you been here?"

"Three months, and I have about three more to go."

"I thought the CDC recommended only three-month hitches."

"They do, but I've already had Ebola. I got it on my first stint. They weren't sure I was going to make it. But everyone got to me early and I was treated right away. They tell me it was touch and go for a while, but I survived, and it means I can't get it again. So I'm an excellent candidate to work here. You, on the other hand, need to be doubly careful. There are other things besides Ebola that can get you. Of course you know about the water, but be sure to always shake out your shoes before putting them on. Spiders and other insects crawl inside." Will practically jumped to his feet. "We need to get back, and I'll show you around."

Dillon stood, his mind racing. There were going to be a lot of things he needed to remember and many things he'd always taken for granted that were simply not going to be there. He hadn't thought about air-conditioning or bugs, or even the basic sanitation that seemed missing outside the hospital complex. He was starting to wonder if he was cut out for this work after all. Up to now, he'd had an easy life. Sure, his parents were distant, but he always had every convenience possible. Even at the hospital, he could get whatever he needed when he needed it. Here he was going to have to make do with what was at hand. Dillon followed Will outside, swallowing hard.

Will began talking right away, and Dillon hurried to catch up. "We monitor everyone's temperature on a regular basis. It's the first sign of Ebola."

"Yes. It's believed that people aren't contagious until the viral load is large enough for the body to manifest a fever."

"That has been our experience, although there have been a few cases that throw that into doubt. However, that was with people who came into very close and intimate contact with an infected person, so they may have been at the tipping point. The thing is, we wash hands religiously and are careful about respiration, although to date there has been no record of the disease spreading through casual contact."

"So if I can ask, who cares directly for the patients?"

"I do and so does the nursing staff. They are survivors who have been trained to care for the sick. The mortality rate is still about 50 percent, but we are working to improve those odds. Since survivors can't get the disease, we use them to take direct care of the patients. I am able to have direct contact, of course."

"So how do we care for patients we can't see?"

"Mostly we develop treatment regimens. I know it seems remote from the patients, but it seems to work, and none of the hospital staff at this facility has contracted the disease. Well, we had one doctor get sick a few months ago, but he caught it out in the community." They approached the hospital, and Will opened the door and held it for him. "We might as well get to work." Dillon nodded and followed Will to a changing room.

It was well after dark, and if Dillon's watch was correct, approaching midnight by the time he finished for the day. He'd seen a number of patients, set a broken arm, and helped a woman give birth. Although the clinic had been originally designed to serve Ebola patients, locals quickly gravitated toward any available health care, and now the clinic staff quarantined the Ebola patients and did what they could for patients with other needs. For the most part it was like any other hospital, except the conditions were primitive. Overall it felt a lot like practicing medicine thirty or more years into the past. Now, there was no one else around, and the hospital area was quiet. Dillon stood outside the door, breathing in the slightly fresher night air. He needed a few minutes to gather his thoughts.

"Quite a first day, wasn't it?" Dr. Patel said from behind him. Dillon started slightly and then calmed again. The head of the hospital wasn't much older than he was, but Dr. Patel's face showed years of experience. "Don't worry, you'll get used to it. Thankfully, the epidemic seems to be entering a slow period right now."

"That's good," Dillon said. He knew that infectious diseases had their ups and downs, and this one wouldn't be any different.

"We'd like to think that we're making headway, but the truth is that we don't know where it comes from, so just as it flared up, it'll die for a while only to flare once again." Dr. Patel leaned against the pole that supported part of the roof. "It's a beautiful country, with the coast, rivers, jungles, and desert all concentrated in a small place. The people of this country have been through hell with two civil wars, and the conflict in Sierra Leone, their leaders encouraging and even helping to fund it, slavery in diamond mines. You name it, these people have seen and survived it."

"Now this disease," Dillon said softly.

"They'll make it through that as well." Dr. Patel pushed away from the pole and walked through the night to his quarters. "You should get some rest. The days don't get any easier."

Dillon walked to his quarters and opened the door. Will stood in the center of the room with a single dim light on, wearing only a small pair of shorts. Dillon's mouth went dry before he could look away. Everything that had been hinted at under Will's clothes was on display in all its glory. Will was no body builder, but he was trim, slightly tanned, and oh so sexy.

"You should get some sleep. There will be plenty of work to do tomorrow." Will lay down on his bed, and Dillon began undressing. He kept his back to Will in order to hide his body's errant reaction. He had read that men who liked men were often castigated in this part of the world, and while he might think Will was attractive, that didn't mean the feeling was mutual. Dillon had to live with the man for three months, so it was best that he keep to himself and not let on what he was feeling. He folded his clothes and lay down on his bed in his shorts. Will turned out the light, and Dillon stared up at the dark ceiling, wondering for the millionth time today if he'd made a good decision or if this was the worst mistake of his life.

"You didn't make a mistake," Will said in the darkness. "Every new person wonders that, but you haven't. You're doing good and helping people who wouldn't get it otherwise. This, what we're here for, is why we went to medical school. We didn't know it at the time, but this is practicing medicine at its purest."

"I guess," Dillon said.

"Of course it is." Will's bed squeaked. "There may not be fancy beds or machines to keep people alive, and the operating room is rudimentary, but it's all functional, and we do real good here." Will sighed. "You're used to having it easy, I'm sure."

"That's not fair. You don't really know me," Dillon protested.

"Sure I do. You work in a fancy, top-of-the-line hospital, your parents have more money than God, and while you went to medical school, you wouldn't have to work a day in your life if you didn't want to, so when the going gets tough, you wonder if it's for you." The venom rolled off Will and seemed to fill the room. "You can always go home—just make a call and you can be on a plane in days. None of the people here have that choice. This is their life, and it's up to us to try to make it better."

"You can get off your high horse now." Dillon rolled onto his side.

"I'm on a high horse…," Will spat, and Dillon wondered just what he was getting at, but Will grew quiet and said nothing more.

"Yeah. You are. We just met today and you're already acting like… I don't know. I thought we might get to be friends." Lord knew he could use one in this place. Everything was different, and there were very few touch points that were familiar. He wasn't a team player by nature, but he figured he'd have to be in a place like this in order to survive. But Will wasn't making it easy at the moment.

"So you're staying?" Will asked.

"Of course I am. I don't know where you got the idea that I was leaving." Dillon narrowed his eyes to try to see in the darkness. "Was this some kind of test?" Will said nothing, and Dillon groaned. "You know, you're being an ass."

"I've been told that on multiple occasions." Dillon heard mirth in Will's voice. Apparently the man had some twisted sense of humor. Dillon liked that. "I'm sure I'll hear it again."

"I bet you will." Dillon shook his head and rolled over on the bed in order to try to get some sleep. "Night." The sounds of the

night invaded the small room as they grew silent. Of course Will
snored. Not too loudly, but just enough that it took Dillon a while to
fall asleep. He wondered what was in store for him. He would only
be here for three months. Surely he could survive for three months,
and then he'd go home and continue his life the way it was before.
At least that was the plan. He'd have the experience he wanted,
complete with additional prestige. Eventually the aches and pains of
the day subsided, Dillon's exhaustion overtook his overworked
mind, and he fell into a deep sleep.

HE WOKE with a start to a pained, haunting wail that entered his
sleep like a ghost. He jumped out of bed, his feet hitting the floor
before he realized what he was doing. "What the hell?" Dillon asked
before he remembered that Will was most likely still asleep.

"Someone has died," Will answered softly. "That's the family
expressing their grief to aid his soul's journey to heaven."

"Oh," Dillon said softly.

"That's a sound you never get used to, no matter how many
times you hear it." Will's bed squeaked, and Dillon saw him sit up.
He sat on the edge, across from Dillon. "Unfortunately, the family is
now at risk because they will try to wash and prepare the body for
burial. As you know, in the case of Ebola, that can spread the
disease."

"Oh, God," Dillon whispered.

"The nurses will explain it to them. They've all learned what it
takes to stop the disease and they're from the same culture, so the
family is more likely to listen to them than they are to us."

"But we're the doctors," Dillon said indignantly.

Will chuckled. "Yes, but we're outsiders, and the nurses are
Liberian. They will explain in a way the family will understand."
The weariness in Will's voice came through clearly. He groaned and
stood up. "I'm going to get dressed and see if I can help them."

Dillon stood and dressed as well. He had a lot to learn, so he
might as well start now. It only took a few seconds to pull on his
clothes and shake out his shoes before slipping them on his feet.
Soon he and Will were walking across the compound to where the

family had gathered. The wailing chant rose and fell over and over again and then slowly came to a stop.

"Please," a woman said as she approached Will. "Please let me have my son." Tears ran down her face, and Will looked to the same nurse Dillon had seen when he'd first arrived. She slowly shook her head.

"We can't. I know you want to prepare him for burial, but that will spread the disease to you and your family. Your other children need you," Will said, and Dillon looked at the rest of the family gathered around their mother.

"We have not been able to see him or...." Her tears continued to flow.

"That's so we can protect you and the rest of your family," the nurse said calmly. "Please go home, and when you have made arrangements, come back and we will give you the body prepared for burial so no one else will get sick."

The woman looked at Will, who nodded. Slowly the small, brokenhearted family turned and walked away.

"Teta, did anyone else in the family have a fever?" Will asked the nurse.

"No, thank the Lord." She looked tired and drawn. "I was able to check all of them yesterday when they came, as well as an hour ago." Her accent was strong, but her words clear. When doing his research, Dillon had been surprised to learn that the primary language of Liberia was English and that it was first settled by freed American slaves.

"Maybe we've stopped the spread in this case," Will said softly. "Thank you for all your help." He absently rubbed the back of his neck, and Dillon had to avert his eyes. "Did you meet Dr. McDowell?"

"She helped me when I first arrived." Dillon would have shaken hands, but she made no effort to, and Dillon thought it best. He'd noticed that casual contact between staff members seemed limited.

"Welcome," she said. "I am sorry I was short with you when you arrived."

"Nothing to apologize for. You were busy." Dillon tried to stifle the yawn that formed, but he couldn't. Dillon wondered if he should go back to bed or if he should check on patients. Will made the decision for him.

"Call if you need anything at all," Will said to Teta and turned to walk back toward their quarters.

"I wasn't sure if we should just get to work," Dillon said.

"There's always more work to do, but sometimes sleep is the best medicine, for them and for us. Get some rest—you're going to need it." Will placed a hand on his shoulder as soon as they entered their room. It didn't remain there long, but it was enough to send heat coursing through Dillon. He was so tempted to shift closer to Will, but the hand slipped away. Dillon didn't move, waiting for what came next, but Will's bed creaked, and Dillon took off his shoes and climbed into his own.

HOT BREATH ghosted over Dillon's lips. A warm hand slipped beneath his shirt, making little circles on his belly. Dillon luxuriated in the feel of that firm, caressing hand. He smiled and slowly reached upward, wrapping his arms around Will's neck, pressing their lips together in a demanding kiss. Will tasted just the way Dillon had thought he would, like the outdoors, as if trees and flowers had coalesced into a man. He whimpered softly as Will's kiss became more demanding and he tweaked Dillon's nipple before starting a slow journey down his chest and over his belly. Will paused at his belt, and when Dillon sucked in his breath, Will continued further, brushing against his cock, encircling him with strong fingers, squeezing delightfully.

"Dillon, are you all right?" A hand pressed to his forehead, and Dillon snapped awake, the dream that had surrounded him so amazingly popping like a soap bubble.

"Yeah," he said breathlessly.

"You were muttering in your sleep and seemed restless." Will removed his hand and stepped back. Dillon instantly missed the gentle touch. "I hated to wake you, but…."

"I'm sorry if I woke you." Dillon took a deep breath, the dream, which had been so deliciously vivid, already fading. "What time is it?"

"About four," Will answered. "Go back to sleep."

Dillon heard Will go back to bed, and he rolled over onto his side away from Will and tried not to center his concentration on where Will had touched him. He wasn't a teenager and had had relationships before. He was just hypersensitive because of the new surroundings and being so far away from everything familiar. At least that was what he told himself as he tried to go back to sleep.

Chapter 3

THE NEXT two days were busy beyond belief. Dillon didn't have time to think about anything other than work. The hospital overflowed with patients of all kinds. Thankfully most of the cases were of the normal variety. The dreaded Ebola seemed to be taking a holiday, at least for now. His third morning at the hospital, Dillon got out of bed, stretched, and grabbed his kit. The hospital had showers, and Dillon intended to head over to clean up. Will was out visiting some of the nearby villages with one of the hospital education programs, so Dillon was on his own. He pushed open the door and stepped outside. The breeze was glorious, and while the heat was already building, the day was bright and filled Dillon with hope.

Cries and shouts reached his ears. Instantly Dillon was on alert. Turning, he saw a group of boys kicking around a ball in an empty flat area at the edge of the hospital grounds. Dillon watched the boys play and found himself wandering over. They had on faded clothes that didn't fit very well, probably ones older brothers had once worn that had been handed down through relatives until they wore completely out, which they looked close to doing. The boys waved when they saw him, and Dillon waved back. He was about to turn around when the ball rolled in his direction. Even the ball had seen better days. Rather than black and white, it was shades of gray and patched in a few places with dull tape. Dillon ran to it and kicked it back. One of the boys stopped it, and play resumed. Dillon wandered closer, watching as they played.

"You play too," one of the boys called.

Dillon hesitated at first, but then set down his bag and raced into the fray. He joined one of the teams, and they instantly began to win. Dillon had played soccer in high school as well as college. He liked to think he was pretty good, but it had been a while. However all the moves he'd had came back to him like it was yesterday. His body wasn't as agile, but the muscle memory was still there, if long buried.

"I'm Kparsi," the boy said. They had been speaking a different language among themselves, but he switched to English. He seemed about fourteen, and the others gathered around. "You are good."

"I'm Dillon," he told them.

"You a doctor?" Kparsi asked, pointing toward the hospital.

"Yes," Dillon answered, and the others backed away, huddling together for a few seconds. Dillon wondered what they were up to.

"You're on Kparsi's team, but we get Topka," one of the boys said, and they broke apart. It seemed Dillon had been included in their game. Kparsi kicked the ball into play, and everyone ran and called to each other. Kparsi kicked the ball to him, and Dillon ran it down the field to make a swift goal, sending it sailing through the sticks stuck in the ground to mark the goal. Dillon threw his arms in the air, and the boys on his team did as well. The others groaned, and someone retrieved the ball. The players got back into position, and when the ball was put back into play, Dillon was guarded closely. He was still able to get in a few good plays.

It wasn't long before his clothes were sweated through and Dillon was thirsty as all get out. He went to his bag and found his bottle, taking a huge drink before returning to play for a little while more. When Dillon had to say good-bye, the boys all waved with grins on their faces. Dillon picked up his bag and headed toward the hospital, their laughter and cries fading as he reached the doors. He paused with his hand on the handle, about to pull it open, but he didn't want to. These boys had very little, and when he was their age, Dillon had had everything money could buy. What amazed him was how happy they seemed. Their laughter and energy had filled him with something Dillon hadn't even known he was missing. Exactly what it was, he couldn't put a word to, but the world seemed a little brighter and maybe a little more hopeful. Yeah, it was probably a stupid notion, but these kids who had next to nothing were happy. Dillon sure as hell hadn't been at their age. Materially, he'd had everything, but the one thing he'd wanted—had always wanted—had been missing then, and it was still missing now.

He went right to the shower area and, remembering Will's warning, dumped out his bag on the counter. A large spider fell out with his shirt and slowly righted itself before scurrying away. Dillon wasn't sure if it was dangerous, but he wasn't interested in finding out firsthand either. He managed to scoop it onto a sheet of paper towel and hurriedly transported it outside before returning to the showers to clean up.

Once he had showered, shaved, and felt fresh once again, Dillon dressed and put his dirty clothes in the bag. He needed to find out about laundry facilities. He'd heard he could do his laundry at the hospital, but he needed to learn more about it. His answer came from Teta, who showed him where the machines that anyone could use were located. Dillon thanked her and wondered how the place would ever get along without her. She seemed to be everywhere.

He returned to his room to get his dirty clothes and started a load of laundry.

"How did your morning go alone?" Will asked as he strode in Dillon's direction.

"I played soccer with some boys and I have a load of laundry in. I guess that's progress. How was the trip to the village?"

Will looked around and then motioned for Dillon to follow him. He led the way to a small office and closed the door. "There's so much fear and misinformation putting people at risk. A woman recovered from Ebola here at the hospital, but the village left her alone and refused to come near her for weeks. She nearly starved until one person took pity on her and left food and water outside her door. That was as close as anyone would get to her. They thought another man had the disease, so they barricaded him in his house." Will shook slightly. "We had suits with us, so we went in and found him. We brought him to the hospital. We think he has malaria, and he's being treated."

"Oh, God," Dillon whispered. "You hear about the fear, but being this close brings it home." He sat in one of the chairs. "We aren't immune to it either. I actually thought about not playing with those boys because one of them might have it. I feel stupid about it now, but...."

"No. It's a real concern for all of us. We have to be careful, and I'm glad you are. Disease doesn't discriminate."

"I know. I'm just saying I know how they might feel, because I did for a few seconds."

"I had the same reaction. But we can't stop living our lives for the entire time we're here. Just like at home, not everyone is infected with a disease, and we can't treat everyone like a pariah. It only feeds their fear. We're careful and we wear protective gear when we're around infected people, but otherwise, we try to limit direct contact because that's how Ebola spreads, especially when we are working with active infections."

"But you got sick," Dillon said softly.

"That was two years ago, before we had developed the methods we use now. If I had it to do over, I would change getting sick, but not helping people or trying to be a part of their lives. And I wouldn't stop living mine," Will said seriously and then stood up. "Come on. We need to get to work. I want to go over some of the treatment regimens we're using and see what you think. You might have some ideas we haven't tried yet." They left the office, and Will led him down to the same room where he'd met Will that first day.

Dr. Granger was there, along with Melanie Foster, a pediatric specialist, and Dr. Patel, who motioned for everyone to take a seat. "As most of you know, we have had remarkable success in treating as well as controlling the spread of Ebola in the area. I think education is helping as well as convincing the local population to wash their hands on a regular basis." Dr. Patel turned to Dillon. "We've been handing out personal hygiene kits with basic items like antibacterial soap. It's amazing how the simple things can make a difference. But there are traditions that go back centuries that, not surprisingly, we are having trouble stopping, such as washing the bodies of the dead." This, Dillon knew firsthand, but he kept quiet and listened as Dr. Patel went over treatment options. Dillon offered some suggestions, but unfortunately didn't have much new to offer.

Neither did the others, and once the meeting broke up, Dillon went back to work, barely stopping for the rest of the day to eat.

"Do you want to go for a walk?" Will asked as they were about to leave the hospital, well after dark. Dillon carried his bag containing his now clean laundry. They dropped it off at the room and then began a slow circuit of the hospital perimeter under the lights. "So what's life like for you back home?"

Dillon sighed. "You pretty much hit it on the head that first night. My parents have a ton of money and I was raised with a huge silver spoon and nothing else.'

"They didn't spend a great deal of time with you?" Will asked.

"No. I had a nanny who spent more time with me than both of my parents combined ever have. I saw my mother and father mostly at dinner. Mom had her charities and clubs, and my father worked all the time. He still does. Neither of them really knows who I am. They keep trying to fix me up with—" Dillon paused when he realized what he was about to say. "They think they have the right to decide my life for me largely for their benefit." Dillon stopped and turned to Will. "What is your family like?"

Will chuckled. "So different from yours. The whole family is rather convoluted. My parents divorced when I was young, and both my mother and father remarried, so I have half brothers and sisters, stepsisters, and stepparents. It's difficult to keep everyone straight, and if I tried to explain it to you, I swear you'd end up with a headache. It's almost enough to give me one. So I'll give you the abbreviated story. I lived with my mother and her second husband, Tim, for a lot of my childhood. Tim was a great dad, and he kept in touch with me even after he and my mom eventually divorced."

"Okay, you're right—that is really convoluted."

"Yeah, it is. They were loud and raucous when we would get together. Some of my half siblings and stepsiblings have married and had kids, so it could be even harder to keep everyone straight. So mostly I considered all of them my brothers and sisters and it was a hell of a lot easier." Will stopped walking.

"Do you get together often?"

Will shrugged and started walking again. "Not anymore. I've been traveling quite a bit since leaving medical school. I did my residency and then wanted to change the world, so I took the job with Doctors Without Borders and have been all over the world. I first came to Liberia two and a half years ago. I caught Ebola on my first visit because… well, I was young, stupid, and thought I was invincible. That proved to be so very wrong. I was out of it for nearly two weeks and spent another couple weeks getting my strength back."

"So I take it there isn't a girlfriend or anything," Dillon said and heard Will pause in his answer. Dillon knew that pause; he'd used it many times himself. "It's okay. You don't need to answer if you aren't comfortable."

Will stopped again and turned toward him, gaze probing deeply into Dillon's. "It isn't a subject that's spoken about here." Will's gaze darted around him. "The people don't understand and have very definite beliefs…."

Dillon took in what Will was saying and wondered if he was truly understanding what he was trying to tell him. His breath caught in his throat, and he stood still next to Will, waiting for him to continue.

"They don't take kindly to people like me, so I rarely talk about that part of my life." Will began walking again, and Dillon wished Will would simply say what he meant. "It's been a while since there was anyone special in my life. Since my first years in medical school, I guess. Of course, with the demands on both of us at that time, our relationship couldn't take the strain. We were together for a year, but…." Will paused again as though he was trying to make a decision. "He and I wanted different things." Dillon heard Will swallow.

"I understand. It's been a while since I've had a boyfriend as well," Dillon whispered. "My mom and dad keep fixing me up with the daughters of my dad's business associates. All of them want to see their little girl married off to a doctor, and apparently any doctor will do."

"Your parents don't know?" Will asked.

"They do and just choose to ignore it to get whatever it is they want. So they fix me up with women and actually somehow expect me to go along with it, because after all I was put on this earth for them. At least that's how they see it."

"Jesus," Will whispered. "That's pretty messed up and so very fifties. My family knows, and of course I'm pretty out when I'm at home, but that isn't very often. And when I'm away… as I said, I don't talk much about that part of my life."

"I see," Dillon said, and they continued their walk around the far side of the hospital before ending up back where they started. "I can't get over how pretty it is here."

"Yeah. I've seen a lot of places, and I like to think that everywhere has its own beauty. I was in the mountains in Central America where it rained all the damn time, but everything was so green and lush you had to stop and look, even in the middle of a downpour. It's like that here. The plants are different and it doesn't rain nearly as much, but the palm trees and other plants…."

"Yeah, it gives the place a tropical-resort kind of feel. That is, if you can…." He stopped because he was about to say something he didn't want overheard or repeated.

"I know what you mean. People pay good money to come to places with weather like this—they just don't come here." Will motioned toward their hut. "We might as well get ready for bed. Work starts early in the morning."

Dillon nodded, hoping that Will meant that as an invitation. But once inside they got ready for bed the same as they had for the past few nights. Will turned out the light, and Dillon got into bed, listening to every sound Will made. Dillon had to remind himself that just because they were two gay men alone in a hut in Africa, that didn't mean that they were going to get together, no matter how much he might wish it.

"Do you ever think about going back to the US to stay? Permanently?" Dillon asked, because he thought he needed to say something.

"Yeah, sometimes. But I like the travel and meeting new people, and out here everyone is as new as it gets. There is so much good I can do." Will sounded idealistic, but Dillon was too old and experienced for more idealism. That was how he truly felt deep down. Dillon nodded in the darkness, feeling grossly inadequate.

"I have to ask. Are you some kind of saint? Devoting your life to others and all that without a care for yourself?"

That got him a chuckle. "God, no. I'm as selfish as anyone. Just wait until we get our next shipment of supplies. I'll steal the marshmallows faster than you can blink."

"Marshmallows?" That seemed a weird item to squirrel away.

"Sure. I love cereal treats, and you have to have marshmallows to make them. The other ingredients we have all the time, but not the marshmallows, so I tend to ferret them away." Will chuckled. "Sometimes it's the little things. What do you miss most?"

"At this point air-conditioning, especially at night, but long-term I don't know what it will be." Dillon propped his head up on his arm. "What about you?"

"Ice cream. Sometimes I crave the stuff. The hospital has a freezer, but getting it here is such a problem. I've thought about making some, but it's such a bother and honestly I'm not much of a cook. But that's what I miss. I know it sounds dumb...."

"I don't think so." Dillon lay back. "I thought I'd miss my house and my friends. I probably will eventually."

Will began to laugh. "You know, in about a month you are going to hate this place. I did at that point in my first assignment. We all do. Nothing will feel like home. Everyone and everything is strange. It's normal and part of that whole culture-shock thing. I actually yelled at one of the nurses at the time, and she was patient and didn't throw a pitcher of water on me, although I'm sure she wanted to. She was the one who told me what was happening and why I was being such an ass to everyone. After that I was okay."

"So you're telling me now."

"Sure. I gotta live with you, so if I can head off any assholeness, it's a win for me. See? No sainthood here." Will laughed and his bed squeaked as he rolled over. "Night, Dillon."

"Good night." Dillon said, rolling over as well and closing his eyes. Sleep was the best thing, and it wasn't long before basic fatigue took over.

Chapter 4

DAYS BEGAN to blur together and quickly turned into a few weeks. Dillon worked—a lot— often until he was so weary all he could do was drop into bed at the end of the day. It reminded him of his residency. But the outbreak that everyone kept expecting and that the entire hospital was primed for didn't materialize. Not that everyone wasn't thrilled. None of them was anxious for anyone to get sick, but it was like waiting for an unwelcome visitor that you knew was going to knock on your door at some point, but you didn't know exactly when. The anticipation was getting to everyone— except Dr. Patel.

"I've been through things like this quite a bit. Take the gifts you're given and be grateful, because tomorrow everything could change," Dr. Patel said and then lifted his eyes. Dillon hoped Dr. Patel hadn't jinxed their luck, but kept quiet.

Since the hospital was quiet, at least for now, Dillon wandered outside. He'd come to get something to eat and wasn't on shift until later in the day. Even though it was early, the heat and sun were intense, and he lifted his water bottle to his lips, taking a deep drink.

"What are you thinking about?" Will asked from behind him.

"Nothing much." He turned in time to catch Will's intense gaze on him before Will looked away. He wanted to ask him about it, but wasn't sure it really mattered. Most nights, unless one of them was working, Dillon went to bed listening to Will, wishing the space between their beds was nonexistent. More than once Dillon had gone to bed first, pretending to be asleep just so he could catch a glimpse of Will as he got ready for bed. Every time he did it, Dillon felt like a voyeur, but he couldn't stop himself from watching. He had been around handsome men most of his life, but something about Will called to him; he just couldn't quite figure out what it was.

"It looks like you have some friends looking for you," Will said, and Dillon followed his gaze to where Kparsi approached with his ball under his arm, Topka and another boy just behind him, their usual smiles absent. As they got closer, Dillon saw the problem. The soccer ball sagged under Kparsi's arm, and Dillon realized it had most likely given up the ghost.

"Can you fix it?" Kparsi asked as he held out the ball to Dillon. "You're a doctor, so you can fix everything."

Will chuckled next to him, and Dillon wondered how being a doctor qualified him as an expert on the repair of soccer balls, but he took it and turned to Will. "Any suggestions on our patient, Doctor?" He turned the ball and easily found the problem. The rubber had split along the one seam, and unfortunately Dillon didn't see a way to fix it.

"I'm afraid it's beyond repair," Will said, and Dillon glanced at the boys, seeing their hope fade. Dillon knew it wasn't like they could just go to the store and get another one. "But there may be something we can do." Will turned and went back inside the hospital. Dillon wondered what on earth Will was up to. The boys seemed puzzled as well, and all three of them stared at each other for a few minutes until Will returned, carrying a paper sack. He handed it to Kparsi. "How about a trade?" Will took the old ball from Dillon as Kparsi opened the bag, his lips curling into a smile that grew in radiance as he looked at them and then pulled a pristine ball from the bag.

"Where did you get that?" Dillon asked with a smile of his own.

"Various groups send donations sometimes, and we got lucky. Go on and have fun, boys," Will said and then turned to him. "You too, Dr. Dillon."

The boys already had the ball on the ground, kicking it between them. "Come on, you could use some fun too," Dillon said, and without thinking, he grabbed Will's hand and dragged him after them.

The soccer game started organically. Once the other boys saw the new ball, they joined in, and soon Dillon found himself on the opposite side from Will, having the time of his life. When one of Kparsi's kicks hit Will on the top of the head and went flying out of bounds, Dillon cackled like a deranged idiot. Will rubbed his head, glaring at Dillon, who knew paybacks were a bitch. They came a few minutes later when Dillon went after the ball and ended up on the ground while Will raced toward the goal. The other team cheered as Will scored, and Dillon picked himself up out of the dirt, brushing off his clothes and watching his team scowl as the other celebrated.

The game continued, and as they played, Dillon found himself guarding Will more and more. It hadn't been his original plan, but he just seemed to gravitate toward him. Will had this energy that was contagious. As they played, the sun began to lower and some of the worst of the heat abated. Other staff from the hospital drifted outside, and soon the game had a small audience cheering, clapping, and yelling encouragement. After an hour of nearly nonstop running, Dillon was done. His clothes were soaked through and he'd chugged nearly a gallon of water. Will hadn't fared much better. Of course the boys were still raring to go, so the two doctors backed away and thanked the boys before Dillon collapsed.

"I wonder if we had that much energy when we were that age," Will asked as he leaned forward, hands on his knees, breathing deeply.

"I doubt I ever did," Dillon commented. He couldn't remember ever being that active. Yeah, he'd played soccer, mostly for fun, but he'd been pretty quiet and bookish. That was what his parents expected. Grades and learning were valued because, as his father said more than once, "I'm not taking care of you for the rest of your life."

"Come on. You never stop moving," Will told him as he straightened up and began moving toward their quarters.

"Huh…." Will had been watching him.

"Yeah. You're always moving, working with patients or helping out the nursing staff when you have time." Will glanced toward Granger. "He'd never do that, but when you're at the hospital, you never stop."

Dillon shrugged. He hadn't given it much thought. He'd simply done what he had before, but here it seemed to be appreciated rather than seen as rocking the boat. "I just want to be part of the team."

"Is that how you were at home?" Will asked as they reached the door.

"God, no. I was all about the patients. And I am here too, but I didn't care what I had to do or who I pissed off to get what I wanted. My patients loved me but reportedly everyone else was... less than pleased to have to deal with me. Not that I noticed or cared."

"So what's different here?" Will stepped inside and Dillon followed.

"I wish I knew. I'd like to say that I've changed, but if I were to go back home, I know I'd go right back to the way I was. Patients need to come first and...." Dillon paused.

Will pulled off his shirt, and Dillon instantly lost his train of thought. He knew he should turn away, but damn. Will was tanned, toned, and fine—not bulky, but fit. He let his gaze flow over him and then to Will's eyes, which burned with intensity. Will turned away first, and reached for his shower bag. Dillon got his own and followed Will out and over to the hospital as though he were the pied piper. He wondered if Will even noticed the way Dillon looked at him. Attraction was a funny thing, in Dillon's experience. He'd been attracted to plenty of guys over the years, and he knew he'd had a lot of guys interested in him.

"You were saying?" Will prompted without turning around.

Dillon tried to pick up his train of thought and failed. Not that it was important anyway, at the moment. He was entranced by the way Will's shoulder muscles flexed and relaxed with the slight swinging of his arms. Will stopped and glanced over his shoulder. Dillon knew he'd been caught midstare and his cheeks colored like a teenager, but he didn't look away. He caught Will's gaze and held it for a few seconds. God, it was intense, with heat that sent a zing up Dillon's back. He didn't notice the approaching footsteps until Will turned away and silently continued down the hall. Dillon blinked a few times to clear his head, wondering just what had happened. Then he once again followed Will around to the shower facilities.

Will had put his shirt back on just before entering the hospital, and after he got fresh clothes from his locker, he disappeared into one of the shower stalls, pulling the curtain closed. Dillon got his clothes as well and took the next one. He undressed and started the water, trying not to think of Will, naked and wet in the next stall. Dillon was afraid he was becoming a little obsessed with Will. He dreamed about him and continually undressed him with his eyes, hopefully when Will wasn't looking. The thing was, Will had to know Dillon was interested in him, though he'd never let on or acted on it. Dillon ran his hands over his face and then down his chest before reaching for the bar of soap. He needed to stop this… preoccupation with the guy he was rooming with for months yet.

Dillon washed his hair and then cleaned himself thoroughly. His cock pointed straight up, bobbing and jumping whenever Will made a sound next door. Taking things in hand crossed Dillon's mind more than once, but he didn't want to take a chance that Will would know what he was doing.

The water shut off in the next stall, and Dillon took a final rinse before turning down the hot water. The blast of cooler water had the desired effect, and Dillon turned off the shower, reaching for his towel. He dried himself and pulled on his underwear and light pants. He pushed the curtain aside and stepped out into the slightly drier air.

The mirrors above the sinks were completely fogged, and Dillon finished drying his hair before grabbing his kit to comb it as best he could. He tried using his towel to wipe the mirror, but that did little good with all the moisture in the air.

It eventually dissipated, and Dillon pulled on his shirt, watching Will out of the corner of his eye, even as he chastised himself for doing it. If Will wasn't interested in anything other than being colleagues and friends, there was nothing Dillon could do about it and he needed to let it be. He told himself that, but his errant body completely ignored him and he still watched Will.

"What time are you on shift?" Will asked without appearing to look at him.

"Half an hour," Dillon answered, and Will nodded without saying anything more. Dillon had figured that as soon as he was done here, he'd head on in and try to get a head start. He had patients he wanted to check up on. "It's been quiet."

Will nodded. "That's good, but it won't stay that way for very long."

"Why do you think that?"

Will scoffed lightly. "In this country there is always something. We're here because they need help, but the government isn't always a friend to its own people. Greed, corruption, and violence all take their toll. Ebola and the other diseases we face here have been around for a long time. With a real effective effort, they could have been controlled and stopped a long time ago, but no effort was made. Those in power were more interested in making money in diamonds and fostering unrest in Sierra Leone and other places because it lined their pockets. Meanwhile the people they were supposed to be helping got worse off, not better."

"But they let us in here," Dillon said as he reached for his socks and shoes. "We're helping."

"They let us in because we don't cost them anything and because the world is watching. Otherwise they would hardly give a damn." Will finished tying his shoes and stood up. "Are you ready? I'm on shift soon as well. I figure I'll get a head start." Apparently their conversation was over.

Dillon was nearly done as well. He tied his last shoe and got up, putting his things away and the dirty towels in the hamper before walking with Will out into the hospital proper.

He was busy for hours, but not frantic. Grateful for that, Dillon spent more time with his patients, especially the younger ones, who seemed pleased to see him whenever he stopped by. This was the part of medicine Dillon loved best—making sure the people in his care had what they needed, and it was obvious that many of them didn't have all they needed on a regular basis. Doya, for example. When Doya had first come in, Dillon thought he was about fourteen, but after asking some questions, it turned out he was nearly eighteen, thin as a rail, and, to Dillon's eyes, stunted, most likely due to malnutrition. It ripped Dillon's heart out and he always brought Doya something extra whenever he came to see him. Not that it would do any good in the long term, because as soon as he left, Doya would be going back to the same environment he'd come from. After staying as long as he could, Dillon left Doya's bedside and walked out of the general ward. He nearly ran into Dr. Patel. Dillon skidded to a halt just in time and excused himself before continuing on outside and into the shade of a palm tree. He needed a few minutes to collect his thoughts.

"You can't be everything to everyone," Will said.

Dillon hadn't heard him approach, the pounding in his ears had been so loud. "Why the fuck not?" he shot back. "These kids don't deserve this. They're just kids. Why isn't everyone more upset?"

"Because we've seen it before and we'll see it again. You live in a city back home, right?" When Dillon nodded, Will continued. "Then you've seen some of the same things come through the hospital doors. Here there's just more of it." Will stepped closer and his voice softened. "It's easy back home to ignore it because we're so busy or we work in a huge hospital and we see relatively few specific patients." Will looked around, and Dillon followed his gaze. "Here we can't get away from it. The need is everywhere."

"But can't we help him?"

Will turned back to Dillon, watching him intently. "Haven't you noticed how big the staff is here? There's a man—a kid, really—who washes all the floors, except the quarantine wards, each and every day. It takes him a few hours, and for that we make sure he gets fed. There are dozens of people like that. Look at this compound. It's picture perfect because there's a man who makes sure it stays like that. Dr. Patel makes sure that man and his children eat here at least once a day. We all have someone who's touched us who we try to help." Will sighed. "It's our way of making a small contribution. If we had our way, we'd open the doors to feed everyone who needed it, but we don't have the resources because in this country, that would mean feeding half the population around us every day. We don't have what it would take to help everyone, but we help those we can."

"It seems so futile sometimes," Dillon said.

"Remember what I told you when you got here? About the frustration and the way you'd hate this place?"

Dillon nodded.

"I think it just hit you early."

"I was always a quick study," Dillon deadpanned.

"And it's not futile. We make a difference by being here and doing our best. Because the hospital is here, the villages around us are healthier and happier. We care for the sick so they can expend their efforts trying to survive and make a living off the land, which they can do under normal circumstances. But here, nothing has been normal in quite a while."

"So what do I do?" It all seemed so overwhelming. Dillon was shocked at how fast everything had settled on him.

"You're doing it," Will said. "You're here. That's how we make a difference. So you need to pick yourself up and put this feeling of futility aside when it shows up—and it will from time to time—and move ahead. I've been doing this for a few years and it still gets to me sometimes. I like to think it's part of our nature. We're doctors and we heal people. We want to help." Will paused. "Back home, professional detachment and all that stuff works well. It's part of how we keep ourselves sane. But here it breaks down. We see these people every day. We live among them, play soccer with them." Will smiled.

"Yeah…." Dillon took a deep breath and followed Will back inside.

Will turned as soon as the door closed. "You didn't sound convinced."

"It's not that."

"Then what? Why did you become a doctor?"

"It seems dumb, but I found out I was good at it. Science, physiology, diagnostics…. I was never very skilled at the things my father thought I should be. He wanted an athlete, and while I played soccer, it was mostly to get him off my back. I played hard to try to make him proud of me." Dillon shrugged. This seemed like a weird time and place for this discussion, but he'd started down the path and it was too late to stop. Thankfully there were few people around. Even so, Dillon stepped off into a small room. "Not that it mattered. By then I'd told them I was gay and that was yet another disappointment."

Will's mouth hung open slightly. "Aren't they proud of you now?"

"I have no idea. Mostly I swear they think of me as bait for one of my father's business deals. 'Sell me your company and your daughter can marry my son. By the way, he's a doctor.'" Dillon rolled his eyes. "They have no idea who I really am, and they don't seem to care."

"At least you aren't bitter," Will said sarcastically.

Dillon chuckled. "Maybe just a little." He turned toward the ward. "I'd hazard a guess that Doya's family cares for him and does their very best. He may not have enough to eat, but it isn't because he'd been neglected. I doubt mine ever cared about me like that, even if I never had to worry about where my next meal was coming from." Dillon sighed once again. "I wonder which of us is truly the better off?"

Will clapped him on the shoulder. "Now you're being maudlin and feeling sorry for yourself. Not pretty, by the way, especially in light of the fact that there are people dying just down the hall."

Dillon couldn't stop his chuckle. "Yeah. That puts things in perspective."

Will nodded. "Let's get back to work so we can continue making a difference. We have people who need us." He flashed a smile, and Dillon nodded and got back to work, but the sense of futility and frustration didn't dissipate as quickly as Dillon had hoped it would.

BY THE time he finished his shift and completed everything he needed to do, it was well after dark, and Dillon walked back to his room. A low light burned in the window, so he knew Will was already there.

"I was wondering when you'd be getting back," Will said softly when Dillon came inside. He was lying on his bed in just a pair of shorts, arms back, hands under his head. The man looked good enough to eat, with his smooth chest and light trail of hair that went from his belly button and disappeared into his shorts. Damn, Dillon wanted to see where it went. But Will didn't move and his eyelids drifted shut. "Is everything okay?"

"Yeah. Doya is doing much better. We're going to discharge him tomorrow."

"So you were sitting with him?"

"Yeah. I had a little time, so we talked and worked one of the puzzles." Dillon had also made sure that Doya ate as much as possible. He knew it wasn't the most rational thing to do, but he wanted him to have a chance. Already Doya looked better, and even after only being with them for a week, he was less drawn and had even filled out somewhat, especially in the face.

"You can't save them all. But I did talk to Patel, and he said that for now, Doya needs to have regular follow-up appointments and that if they were to be around mealtimes, then…."

"Thanks," Dillon said and began getting ready for bed. He was so tired his eyelids felt like concrete. He was under no illusions that this was some sort of solution, but at least he would be able to check in on Doya for the near future. He'd cleaned up pretty well before leaving the hospital, so he turned out the light and got undressed before getting into bed. Dillon heard Will doing the same thing. Then the room was quiet. Will's bed protested when he rolled onto his side. Dillon did the same, staring at Will's back in the near darkness. He was just a shape, but Dillon knew he was there and his scent filled the room. He inhaled and ended up rolling onto his other side so the scent would lessen and he'd be able to go to sleep.

"Night," Will said, and Dillon returned the sentiment before closing his eyes, wishing he could somehow put an end to this torture. Part of him wanted to get up and go right over to Will's bed, join him, and kiss away any resistance until Will begged and writhed with need. Hell, Dillon was damn near that now just at the thought, but he eventually managed to drop off to sleep.

Chapter 5

THE WAILS of grief began early in the morning about a week later, only these weren't coming from the hospital. Will was already up and on his feet. Dillon got up as well. They'd had what Will described as another week of quiet, but he got the distinct feeling that the quiet was over. Granted, this could be a natural death, but as the sound got closer, Dillon knew this was nothing ordinary. As soon as he was dressed, he stepped outside behind Will, and they both hurried over to the hospital.

"I'm going to go see what's up," Will said. "You put on one of the clean suits and meet me near the isolation ward."

"How do you know what it is?"

"Just a feeling," Will called, already hurrying toward the sound. Dillon did as Will instructed, putting on the full body suit, gloves, and mask, instantly sweating like a pig. It was better than becoming another victim of this epidemic, though. Sure enough, by the time he reached the area, nurses and doctors were taking in patients and settling others into temporary living quarters.

"What happened?"

"The father works most of the week at a tire factory outside Monrovia. He came home to visit the family a few days ago and hid his symptoms at first. Unfortunately he didn't come in then, and his family initially tried to treat him themselves, so now the entire family and part of the village has been exposed. So we're going to put up the highest-risk people here and have the rest of the villagers quarantined. But that can be brutal, because no one will go anywhere near them." Will sounded haggard. "Let's get everyone settled."

"What about the man who has it?"

Will's expression went very somber. "That's who they were mourning. The morgue will have the body prepared so there's no additional spreading, but the damage has been done."

"I'll go help settle people," Dillon said. "Do I need this suit?"

"Probably not, but stay safe. Minimize direct contact, in any case, and wear a gown and mask. He was home a few weeks ago, so we don't know how long he's been contagious or where he contracted it. Dr. Patel is contacting the factory to let them know what we have. They will need to warn their other employees." Will sighed. "This is usually how things start, and then they progress. One person not paying attention can infect dozens of others." Will turned back to what he was doing, and Dillon walked toward the temporary quarters. It was basically a set of small rooms off, but separate from, the isolation ward where a few dozen people could stay both segregated from the isolation ward and largely from each other. The trick was to keep the virus from spreading if one of the isolatees was infected.

When Dillon entered the area, it was pandemonium, people talking over each other, asking what was going on. Dillon explained everything as best he could and tried to settle them down. None were very happy about leaving their homes, but they seemed to understand that this was for their safety and for that of their neighbors. Dillon listened to all of them in turn and helped get them settled. When he got to the last room, he peered in and stopped cold. Kparsi and Topka, along with another of the boys he'd played soccer with but whose name he hadn't caught, stared back at him.

"Hi, Dr. Dillon," Kparsi said, looking at him with intensely sad eyes. The ball they'd all played with sat on the floor near the bed.

"What happened?" Dillon asked.

"Our dad came home and got sick," the boy sitting next to Kparsi said.

"This is my brother, Wamah. You didn't meet him when we played," Kparsi explained. "Topka is our... cousin." He hesitated slightly, searching for the word. Dillon had learned that while the official language of the country was English and many people spoke it because it was taught in schools, tribal languages and dialects were generally spoken in the home, which sometimes created an interesting mix of words and meanings.

"I'm sorry about your father," Dillon said, wondering what else he could say. "We'll try to keep you comfortable here for a few weeks. We want to make sure that none of you contract Ebola, and if you do, we can treat you quickly." It sounded like a standard, rote speech by now, especially in light of the fact that these kids were his friends… of a sort, anyway.

"Can we go outside?" Topka asked.

"Of course," Dillon answered, "but you need to stay away from other people for a while, just until we're sure all of you are healthy." Dillon smiled. "I see you brought the ball." The boys forced smiles and nodded, their misery and worry not abating at all. Not that he could blame them. They had decided to keep the boys together because of equal limited exposure and because it would be easier on them to have each other's support.

Without knowing what else to do, he said good-bye and left the area. He took off the protective suit and washed it down with bleach water to kill off any possible contamination before hanging it up. When he lifted his gaze, he saw Dr. Patel watching him. Dillon turned away and went to the sinks to wash his hands. He did it so many times each day he rarely thought about it. All the reports he'd read explained that Ebola was not transmitted through airborne means, but he could still feel concern well up inside him. When he finished, Dillon rinsed his mouth with mouthwash and then stared at himself in the mirror before making himself go back to work. There were people who needed him, so breaking down was not an option. Up until that moment, Ebola and its victims had been abstract, but seeing those three boys he knew and had played soccer with put a face on the disease he hadn't been expecting. They'd lost a father and uncle, someone who provided and took care of them. Now there was just the mother and aunt who'd been in the next room, looking equally scared and lost.

Dillon went back to work and didn't see Will or most of the other doctors for the rest of the day. Patients were being checked into the isolation ward, but he knew he needed to stay away and make sure his other patients were comfortable. When he'd come here, Dillon had expected to be working almost strictly with Ebola patients, but instead he'd been fighting other diseases, including malaria and dysentery, as well as run-of-the-mill broken bones and injuries. One of his patients had fallen out of a palm tree. He wasn't out of the woods yet, but he was improving.

By the end of the day, Dillon realized he'd missed lunch and was in danger of skipping dinner as well. The other doctors were swamped with other cases, so he'd picked up the slack. He had been hoping to work with Ebola patients directly, and a few times a little professional jealousy crept in, but he had to remember that he was part of a team. That was what he'd come here to learn, and if he did his job to the best of his ability, then others could do the same. He was just anxious to get into the fray. Dr. Granger came on duty after dark and relieved him. Dillon reviewed all the cases with him and then left for his room.

He got halfway there and turned around, heading to the quarantine area. He put on a mask and gown before entering. Many of the room doors were closed, but the three boys' room was open. Dillon peeked inside, and three sets of saucer eyes looked back at him. Dillon still didn't know what to say to any of them. "How are you boys holding up?" As soon as the words were out of his mouth, he hoped they understood what he meant.

"We're okay," Topka answered softly. "We are fighters."

"I know you are." These boys had seen so much already in their short lives. When Dillon was their age, his biggest worry had been fighting with his parents and getting them to let him stay up past ten o'clock. It hadn't been wondering how they were going to live now that the breadwinner was gone… or worse, if they'd contracted a disease that could kill them. Dillon stood in the doorway, speechless, as all this rammed into him like a blast of wind, threatening to knock him back on his butt. "I promise I'll stop by as much as I can, and if you need something, please ask." God, his words sounded lame as hell. These kids were grieving, with an added dose of fear heaped on the top. Hell, Dillon was afraid for them. The thought of seeing any of them—He slammed the door closed on that thought. "I'll see all of you tomorrow." He wished there was more he could do.

Dillon raised his hand in good-bye and quietly walked out of the isolation area. He took off the mask and gown and tossed them away. Then he left the hospital to go back to his room. Will was there, but Dillon barely acknowledged him. Instead he flopped down on his bed and stared up at the ceiling beams.

"You okay?" Will asked after a while.

"Yeah," Dillon answered automatically. "I just stopped in to see the boys. They're really shaken up."

"Of course they are. But they've seen this before," Will said.

Dillon sat right up and stared down at Will. "I never picked you for heartless. They lost their uncle and father. That only happens once. How can they have seen this before? A part of their world just came crashing down around them."

"I didn't mean it that way." Will sat up. "It did sound like I don't care, but I do. It's just that I can't let myself get involved with all the cases that come through, and you shouldn't either. Help them all you can, but don't let yourself get too emotionally attached."

For some reason this conversation wasn't one he expected to be having with Will. Dillon had expected Will to be more open, and he wondered where this sudden chill had come from. Will hadn't acted like that before. "You're lecturing me on professional distance?" Dillon asked tilting his head slightly. "Because I felt something for… not a patient, but three kids who may have lost the person who provided for them?"

Will stood and walked over to him. "Yeah, I am. What would you know about living from hand to mouth? You never had to worry about a meal in your life."

Dillon jumped to his feet as well, staring Will down. "Doesn't mean I can't feel for them. Hell, at least I'm capable of having feelings." He shivered for effect. "The chill coming off you is better than air-conditioning. What's that about, anyway? You've been helpful for weeks and suddenly you're as cold as a witch's tit. What gives?"

"Nothing. I'm only saying to be careful. God…."

Dillon wasn't buying it, especially given the way Will chewed his lower lip. There was more to this than Will was letting on, and Dillon wasn't sure if he should push or not. He decided that Will would sidestep it if he wasn't ready, so he moved back slightly. "Careful is one thing, but cold is quite another. I never pegged you as chill, so...." Dillon verbally backed up, but he locked his gaze on Will's. The hardness in his expression slowly slipped away. Embers stoked behind his eyes, and Dillon saw some of the heat he'd literally dreamed about. Dillon hesitated, but Will moved his head a hair closer, his lips parted, and his pink tongue flicked slowly over his bottom lip ever so slightly. Dillon's heart did this little flip jump, but he still hesitated.

"I'm not cold," Will whispered with a hint of seduction.

"No. You're hot." Dillon raised his hand, and without actually touching Will, he felt heat roll off him. A tingle started at the back of his neck and went up and down at the same time. He quivered slightly, the sensation forcing his eyes closed for just a second. When he opened them again, Will seemed closer, hotter, and his tongue made an appearance again, gliding slowly over his upper lip.

"What are you waiting for?" Will whispered. "I've been trying to signal my interest for weeks."

Dillon stepped back. "Then why didn't you do anything? You said all that stuff about how people here didn't like people like us, so... I... well, I was waiting for you." Dillon could have laughed at the whole thing except that Will was now too close.

Will slipped his hand around the back of Dillon's neck, rough from hundreds of hand washings, but warm, tugging him closer until his lips touched Dillon's. Dillon wasn't sure what he'd been expecting. He'd dreamed of this first intimate touch, but in his mind it was explosive. Instead, this was slow and warm rather than instant incineration. Dillon liked it and pressed more firmly. Will went right along with him, tilting his head slightly, deepening the kiss while pushing Dillon back. It was hard to believe that Will was with him like this. He'd thought about it so much that he'd started to think he'd completely jinxed it and this would never happen.

"Umfff." The back of Dillon's legs bumped the side of his bed and he had to stop himself from tumbling backward. Once he had his balance back, he reached for Will and poured his weeks of frustration into the kiss, tugging on Will's lower lip, tasting his tangy earthiness. Will pressed him back harder, and Dillon began to fall—not freely, but under Will's control. He landed gently on the mattress with Will above him, his heated gaze burning into him.

If it were possible, Dillon's clothes would have burned away under the searing passion in Will's eyes. The intensity sent a quiver through Dillon. Never in his life had he been the subject of a look so penetrating that he wondered if Will could see the very beats of his heart. Rather than going up in smoke, Will tugged at Dillon's shirt, exposing his belly and chest to the increasing heat that surrounded them. Will leaned over, pushing his shirt to his neck and then licking his skin with small light touches of wet heat that sent little tongues of white light racing to Dillon's brain. Dillon held his breath, his eyes drifting closed so he could take in the amazing sensation. When Will turned his attention to one of his nipples, Dillon gasped softly.

"Sensitive," Will whispered and sucked wetly once again.

"Oh, God yes," Dillon muttered half under his breath, hoping like hell Will wouldn't stop. But Will did just that, taking time to tug Dillon's shirt over his head before moving him down once again with just the force of his magic lips and tongue. At least they felt magical to Dillon. He knew his nipples were sensitive, but damn, with Will they seemed to have forged a direct line to his dick, which strained against his pants, and Dillon hoped like hell the fabric held against the onslaught. Well, hell, if it didn't, at least the pressure from confinement would be released, and he needed that so damn bad he could hardly catch his breath.

"Damn, you taste good," Will mumbled and then lightly scraped his teeth over sensitive skin, sending Dillon into erotic orbit. He gripped Will's cheeks and guided him up to his lips. He'd intended to take possession of Will's lips to try to gain a modicum of control over this encounter, but Will ripped that away and left Dillon panting for more.

"I take it you like to be in control," Dillon whispered.

"Oh, yeah," Will moaned, and Dillon got the idea there was a story behind those few words. He wanted to know what it was, but not now. Instead, he wrapped his arms around Will's neck and tugged him closer. If Will wanted control, Dillon could give it to him. Hell, as long as he continued the mind-blowing heat, he could have control forever. Somehow Dillon got Will's shirt open, and they both sighed when their chests mashed together for the first time. The room heated quickly, and Dillon adored it. He ground his hips upward, clutching at Will's ass through his pants, pressing his cock to the ridge of Will's.

Their moans melded and mixed as they kissed and held each other. Dillon sighed when Will tugged at his belt and then yanked his pants open. The release of pressure was so amazingly welcome he could barely describe it. Dillon pulled at Will's pants, and once he got them open, he slid his hands beneath the waistband and down to cup Will's butt cheeks. He was firm all over, and Dillon grasped the muscle as it flexed and relaxed with the movements of his hips.

Will lifted himself off Dillon and stood by the edge of the bed. "You look debauched already." Will grasped the legs of Dillon's pants and tugged them off, throwing them over the back of the chair before stepping out of his own. Dillon shucked his boxers while Will did the same. Then he stared at Will, drinking him in with relish like a cool glass of water on a hot day. Will looked almost exactly as Dillon imagined him: lean, strong, but not bulky, with honey-colored smooth skin and a light trail from his belly button that led to treasure. Will's cock jutted toward him, thick and long. Dillon's mouth watered and he licked his lips in anticipation. Without thinking, he leaned closer, opened his mouth, and extended his tongue. Will didn't move, and Dillon took his first intimate taste.

Damn! Will's taste burst on his tongue from that first light lick. Dillon sat up and ran his hands over Will's hips and around to his butt. He pressed him forward and slowly sucked Will between his lips.

"Damn," Will whispered and let Dillon suck him deeper. Dillon took all he could, relaxing his throat, loving every amazing inch as it slid over his tongue. He was in no hurry and slowed his pace, tugging on Will's cock as he pushed his lips down the shaft. Will moaned and stifled it, his cock jumping slightly in excitement. Dillon sucked him deep and the moaning got louder. "God…."

Dillon smiled around Will's cock and continued sucking him. He adored the chorus of sounds Will made. He wondered how long it had been since Will had been with anyone, but he wasn't going to stop to ask those kind of questions now.

Will thrust his hips slowly, and Dillon stroked his own cock to the time of their movements. Then, without much warning, Will pulled away and pushed Dillon back onto the bed. He kissed him hard, and Dillon held Will tightly, twining their legs together as he moved his hips, desperate for sensation. His body felt like it was on fire, and while Will was the source, only he had the ability to quench the heat. Will scooted him upward on the small bed until Dillon was comfortable. Then he gently held Dillon down by placing an arm over his chest. Dillon wondered what was coming and gasped when Will sucked him into the hottest wetness he had ever imagined.

Dillon swallowed hard. "Suck me," Dillon whispered. He wanted to reach for Will's head and thrust him down on his cock, hard. His body screamed to go for it, balls to the wall, but Will had other ideas and held him back.

"Oh, yeah," Will whispered and took Dillon hard once again.

Dillon's eyes crossed and he closed them, letting wave after wave of ecstasy break over him. He was getting damn close and all he could do was whimper a warning. Speech was beyond his abilities right then and he could have cared less. Will backed away and crashed their lips together. It would have been painful if Dillon had actually cared, but as it was, the intensity was mind-blowing. "Do you have supplies?" Dillon managed to gap between breaths.

"Is that what you want?"

"Fuck yeah." Dillon was consumed with unrelenting anticipation.

Will's weight disappeared, and Dillon heard him rummaging in one of his drawers. The heat between them settled slightly, but as soon as Will touched him, it returned with a vengeance. "How long has it been?"

"A while," Dillon whispered, forcing his mind not to take him there at this moment.

"Then roll over. It'll be easier and I won't hurt you."

Dillon groaned but took Will's suggestion. As soon as he settled, Will pressed to him, back to chest, sliding his cock along Dillon's cleft, reminding him just how much of a big boy he was.

"Damn, you're huge." For a second, Dillon wondered if he was too large, but he wanted him. He'd dreamed about him and wasn't going to let a little trepidation get the better of him.

"Don't worry. I'll go slow and make it good."

Dillon arched his back and turned his head so he could see Will. "I know you will." They kissed sloppily, and when Will's lips left his, they transferred to his shoulder and then Will kissed down the center of his back, his hot hands following behind. Small trembles of delight went up and down him. Dillon wasn't sure if he should move or not. Finally he gave in and pushed back into Will's gentle touch as he slid into the small of his back and then farther down to his butt.

Will kneaded and licked his cheeks. "Damn, you're something else."

"What do you mean?" Dillon asked, moving into the touch, needing more.

"I would have guessed that you would have been thoughtful and precise in bed, but you're such a hedonist. Every touch seems to light up something inside you. It's heady, to say the least. Are you always like this?"

"I don't think so," Dillon gasped when Will scraped his teeth over a cheek, chuckling softly.

"That's even better. So this is all for me." Will seemed thrilled and sucked on one cheek.

"What are you doing?"

"Marking you a little." Will continued sucking. "Don't worry, no one will see it, but I'll know it's there." He licked and sucked for a while, and Dillon wondered if his entire ass was going to be black and blue. Not that it mattered. When Will made his way deliciously up his back, Dillon shook with excitement. Will sucked at the base of his neck and rubbed his cock between his cheeks. Dillon kept waiting for Will to prepare him, but he seemed content to take his time. When he finally did, Dillon's breath escaped him. Even Will's fingers were thick and long, filling and emptying him until Dillon could hardly think. Then, and only then, did Dillon hear the telltale rip of foil followed by a hesitation before Will's cock pressed to his entrance and paused.

"It's okay," Dillon whispered.

Will worked his arms beneath Dillon's chest, holding him tight. Dillon lifted his hips and pressed back, pushing until the tip of Will's cock pressed inside him. The feeling took his breath away. He gasped loudly and stilled. God, he needed time to adjust. His head was on fire and his body… it was indescribable and nearly overwhelming. When Will pressed deeper and the initial shock wore off, the discomfort morphed into pleasure as big as Will was.

"Oh, God," Dillon moaned as Will slid deeper and deeper, filling him in a way he'd never thought possible. When Will pressed his hips to his ass and stilled, Dillon sighed. When he moved again, Dillon moaned softly, but with each subsequent movement, his exclamations became louder and more forceful. He knew he needed to quiet. The last thing he wanted was others to hear him, but damn, he could hardly control anything at this point.

Will withdrew, and Dillon held his breath, releasing it when Will slid back into him, long and slow, in a graceful movement that took him from empty to full in seconds. "God," he groaned loud and long. Will seemed to love it because he did it again… and again. Then he grasped Dillon's shoulder and drove into him, scraping over that spot inside so many times that Dillon could barely think. All he did was extend his hands under the pillow, grab the headrail of the steel bed, and hold on.

Will withdrew once again and his weight shifted. He tapped Dillon on the hip, and he rolled over. Will lifted Dillon's legs and gave him time to get comfortable before slowly entering him once again.

Seeing Will's eyes, deep and strikingly dark, made all the difference in the world. Where before the sex had been great, now it was even more intense. Each movement had meaning as Dillon locked his gaze on Will's, touched the center of his chest, and felt a rightness flow over him. This was what life was supposed to feel like, how being with another was meant to be. In those few minutes, things seemed to become clear for him.

Will wrapped his fingers around Dillon's cock, gripping hard and stroking fast. One thing Dillon wished he could understand was why another man's hand on his cock felt different from his own. Well, not just different, but more.

"Yes! Don't stop."

"I won't." Will paused and leaned over him, kissing him hard while making small movements with his hips. "I never want to stop."

The pace quickened and the bed rocked. Dillon went wild and felt incredible. He held on as Will took him higher. Soon Dillon seemed to be viewing himself from the top of a mountain, surrounded by clouds at the peak of barely controlled ecstasy. Then it came to a stop and the cloud cleared until only he and Will remained.

"You left me for a minute," Will whispered as he stroked Dillon's chest.

"No. I was with you the entire time," Dillon said, and Will smiled and resumed driving Dillon out of his mind. Seconds became moments and then minutes of unimaginable passion that Dillon wished would last forever. Of course he couldn't, and when he lost control of the last thread that held him, it broke and Dillon tumbled into a release that left him breathless and back floating on those white, puffy clouds once again. This time Will was with him, holding him, kissing him lightly, and it was real, not some illusion of passion. Will was there. Dillon held on, wishing this feeling would remain forever. But slowly it dissipated around them until there was just Will.

Dillon kissed him and relaxed back on the mattress, completely spent and unbelievably happy. "That was... wow." He smiled and when he opened his eyes, Will looked right back at him, brown eyes as deep as night.

"You can say that again," Will breathed and shifted slowly. Their bodies separated, and Will carefully got off the bed. He took care of the necessary items and then returned. Dillon reached for his shirt and used it to wipe himself up. Then he tossed it aside and made room, as much as he could in the small bed, for Will. "I didn't think you were interested."

Will chuckled. "And I thought you weren't interested. I should have known that was wrong by the way you kept looking at me, but I wasn't sure and...." Will paused. "I've never had good instincts about things like that."

"Why do you say that?"

"Well, I... when I was in college, I was interested in a guy. We lived in the same dorm and he was really cute. He used to work a room like no one's business, and he always seemed to touch me. They were just light taps on the shoulder, that kind of thing, but I thought they meant more than they did. When I approached him to see if he was interested in me, I ended up walking in on him and his girlfriend. It was really embarrassing." Will chuckled and then began to laugh. Dillon joined in with him. "I suppose it could have been worse."

"Yeah," Dillon said. "At least he didn't threaten to kick your ass because you made a pass at a straight guy. That happened to me once. It was in a gay bar, no less. Apparently this guy had been brought by his girlfriend because she wanted to see what it was like, and when I approached him, he went a little nuts. Of course all the other guys in the place made him feel pretty stupid." Dillon sighed as his chuckles diminished. "Leave it to me to be in a room full of gay men and ask the only straight one in the place to dance."

Will began to laugh again. "I guess we're a pair. It seems to work out for both of us."

"Yeah, and we learned our lessons, maybe a little too well." Dillon hugged Will a little tighter.

"You know we have to be careful outside this room," Will said, and Dillon nodded. "That is, if you want more than what just happened."

Dillon stilled. "Do you?" Will sighed and Dillon unlocked his hands and let them fall back to his side. "I have terrible luck with any sort of relationship. The life I lead isn't very conducive to anything long-term. I go from camp to camp, wherever I'm needed." He shrugged. "That's been my life for the past three years, and I really love it."

"I understand," Dillon whispered hoping like hell he'd kept the disappointment out of his voice. He'd gotten carried away, and since they were so good together, he'd let himself think there could be more to it. But Will had shut that idea down in a hurry.

Will stared at him, gaze probing. "No, you don't. What you just heard was that I wasn't interested in you, and that's not what I said."

"How?"

"I saw some of the light go out in your eyes." Will shook his head. "All I'm saying is that I don't know what I want or what's going to happen. I'm not sure I'm capable of having a normal relationship."

Dillon rolled onto his side and propped his head up on his arm. "Why?" Will was quiet and Dillon wasn't sure he was going to get an answer.

"I didn't have the best home life. I had no good examples of lasting relationships from my parents or stepparents."

Dillon scoffed. "Mine were cold, distant, and selfish, so we have something in common when it comes to family."

"You said something like that before, but it couldn't be that bad."

"It was. We might have had money, but that was all I had. Everything that money could buy, but very little else. At the time I thought it was normal—until I got to school and saw my friends with healthier relationships."

"Why did you become a doctor?" Will asked, and Dillon figured it was a way for Will to change the subject.

"I was always good in school and certain things came easy to me. But I had this friend—his name was Josh. I used to go over to his house a lot. He had sleepovers and his mom made real dinners. I actually thought that everyone else ate alone in the dining room at their own big table. It wasn't until I was at Josh's that I saw how real families ate together. He was like a brother to me and my best friend. That is until he turned fifteen and caught a cold that turned into pneumonia, and then the infection spread further. The doctors messed something up in his treatment and the infection spread to his brain. After that he didn't last very long. I remember sitting in the chair next to his hospital bed. I'd snuck out of the house and conned the driver into taking me to the hospital. Josh's mom had told me he wasn't doing very well, and I had to see him. The nurses tried to kick me out, but I dropped my dad's name and they left me alone. I guess he was good for something." Dillon closed his eyes. He could remember the smell of the room, the dim light, how ashen Josh was when he walked in. Dillon had sat in the chair just to be with his friend.

"I guess I stayed about an hour, until my mom freaked out and came to get me. She was so mad, but I didn't care, especially after Josh died the next day. He was my best friend and only fifteen, and he was gone. When my dad tried to punish me for leaving the house, I called him every name I could think of and told him Josh was dead. That's the only time I remember my dad being speechless. I left the room and went into the library we had and began reading every book on medicine I could find." Dillon took a deep breath. "Josh had given me a Mustang car model for my twelfth birthday, one of those cast metal ones. It was really cool and everything worked—the doors, steering wheel, all of it. He and I put it together, painted it and everything. I brought it to the funeral home and put it in the casket when no one was looking." Dillon's eyes filled with tears and he blinked them away. "I figured he died before he got to drive a car, so at least he could drive that one." Dillon wiped his eyes. "I usually have some bullshit answer ready for people who ask me that question, but I became a doctor for Josh, and I chose my specialty because of him too."

"What do you think Josh would think of you being over here?" Will asked.

"I don't know. I'd like to think Josh would say it was cool and ask me to bring a palm tree back for him. He was into plants and turned his folks' backyard into a huge flower bed. He had everything out there, and his room was filled with stands and grow lights. So he'd want a palm tree or some exotic plant for his collection that, of course, I wouldn't be allowed to bring into the US...." Dillon realized he was rambling, but he didn't much care.

"Why did you become a doctor?" Dillon asked after a minute.

Will laughed. "My mom pushed me to medical school. She said I was smart and that if I wanted out of where we were living, I needed to get an education. It was the only important thing to her. When I got my bachelor's degree, she said I should apply for med school. I thought she was nuts, but did it anyway. I'd always been interested, but there was no way I could afford it. I got a scholarship and then a second one. It seemed I qualified for just about everything. I took out loans to pay for the rest and here I am. Most of them are paid off because of my service here and other places. That's a side benefit to working in places most people won't, and in a year, I'll be done."

"Is that why you stay?"

"No." Will didn't elaborate, and Dillon didn't think he would get much more out of him. Dillon could see him shutting down and he wondered what could be so bad. Was Will running away from something? The possibilities raced through his head and Dillon had to stop them. It had to be his imagination going on overdrive. "I love what I do," Will finally added. It was a pat answer and one Dillon understood, but didn't truly buy.

"I can see that, but there has to be more to it." There was a story there; Dillon could feel it.

"There's isn't some grand story or huge intrigue. I'm not running away from anything." Will paused and shifted nervously. Dillon slid his hand over Will's side and around to his belly, holding him closer. It was warm, but it didn't matter. Will felt good against him. "There's just nothing for me to go back to. My family is a mess. My parents divorced and my mother remarried and then divorced again, so I have siblings, half siblings. They all have their lives and new families. At some point my mother found religion and she went full bore with it. They helped her get her life on track in a way, but when I told her I was gay, she pretty much said that I should pray for God to heal me." He shrugged and made this cute gesture with his lips.

"So you're saying your family won't accept you, no matter what?" Dillon said.

"I doubt it. I don't talk to my mother very often, and lately when I do, it's like we're total strangers."

"You've been gone for years. When was the last time you saw each other?" Dillon closed his eyes and lay there. He'd always thought his family was messed up, but things seemed worse with Will's. His family was obtuse and self-centered, but at least he knew his folks would be there in the end, if for no other reason than that they'd worry how it would look to other people.

"It's been a while. The last time I had a break between assignments, I bummed around Europe for a few months. I had a lot of fun and saw all kinds of places." Will moved away and slowly rolled over. "When I was in school, my mom, in particular, was very supportive, but as soon as I came out, all that changed. I knew she was going to have a problem with me being gay with the newfound religious fervor and all, so I kept putting off telling her until I realized she didn't know who I was anymore. So one day I came home and told her."

"Did you have a boyfriend at the time?"

"No. There wasn't anything that prompted it other than the fact that we were growing apart. Mom was all about honesty and truth. At least that's what she said, but she wasn't interested in that when it came to me being gay." Will sighed, and Dillon saw massive amounts of pain well in his eyes. He could almost reach out and touch it. "She wanted me to deny who I was and live a 'normal' life. She even offered to arrange a marriage for me. My mom is Italian, and she said she'd find an old-fashioned matchmaker to arrange a wife. I was floored. That wasn't how I was raised, but suddenly everything I thought I knew about my mom had changed."

"I'm sorry. My folks aren't the greatest, but they are who they are." Dillon was quickly realizing that maybe he hadn't had it so bad after all.

"After that I was on my own and I needed to make a change in my life. I'd always wanted to travel and looked into options... the rest is history." Will looked tired. Dillon inched forward and kissed him lightly. "I should go to my own bed. There isn't enough room for both of us to share one of these."

Will got up, and Dillon missed his closeness. He knew Will was right, but it felt like they were separating way too soon. Will had bared a part of himself that Dillon knew in his heart he didn't talk about with anyone. Having him go to his own bed just seemed wrong somehow. Will turned out the light, and Dillon heard the familiar soft squeak as he lay down.

He sighed and stared up at the ceiling for a long time. "Will, you asleep?" Dillon asked in a very soft whisper.

"No."

Dillon sighed and got out of bed. He pulled at the footboard and slid the metal-framed bed toward Will. Then he got behind it and pushed the bed the rest of the way until they were side by side. Then he lay back down and reached over, locating Will's hand and taking it in his.

"You're something else, you know that?" Will whispered with a touch of lightness in his voice that hadn't been there before.

"So are you, and for the record, if your family knew the man I know from the past few weeks, they would be very proud of you." Dammit, Will had spent his life helping people less fortunate than him! Dillon had come over with an agenda, hoping this experience would look good on his resume.

"Well, I can't change their minds." The resignation in Will's voice pushed away the happiness that had been there a few seconds earlier. "I had to realize I can't change the way they feel. I tried and failed, so I dealt with what I have to."

Except Dillon got the idea Will wasn't dealing with it, or at least he didn't seem to be. "Have you thought of going back to see your family again?"

Will shrugged. "Maybe. I really don't know. Maybe it would be worth it. My biological parents haven't seen me in a while. But I also think they could have just written me off as a failure and moved on. I was never close to my father and am estranged from my mother. I'm grateful for Tim's presence when I was a child, as well as the chaotic crew that are my siblings and their children, but the key relationship, the one between a son and his parents, is deeply flawed."

Dillon wondered how anyone could do that, but pursuing this conversation wasn't going to get either of them anywhere. They both had a long day ahead of them and needed sleep. Dillon moved closer to Will, stroking lightly up his chest and neck, following the curve of his jaw to his lips.

Dillon moved closer and gently pressed his lips to Will's. "There's nothing you can do about it now, and I'm sorry for bringing it up." He kissed him again. "It isn't like I have all the parental relationship answers."

"It isn't like I haven't thought of it before." Will returned his kiss and said good night. Dillon lay back down and fell asleep, still holding Will's hand.

Chapter 6

EACH OF the next few days, Dillon visited his young friends in the quarantine wards. Their spirits did improve once Kparsi's father was buried and the healing could truly begin. Dillon arranged for them to play outside, but he couldn't play with them and had to limit his time and exposure as a precaution. Slowly, the ward emptied as tests for the disease came back negative and it was determined how limited some people's contact had been with the victim. It was largely a lonely existence, and Dillon did what he could to help break the monotony for them. Will helped as well, especially since he was immune to Ebola and could have closer contact without fear of transmission.

"What do you have planned?" Will asked as they left their quarters for the hospital. Dillon couldn't keep the smile from his face no matter how hard he tried. He and Will had rearranged the room so their beds were permanently closer together. As a result they had more space, and if anyone went inside, it would seem as though they had made the change for efficiency.

"Just work. I thought we'd stop by and see the boys, of course. They're going crazy with inactivity. Yesterday I looked into the ward and caught them playing soccer in one of the empty hallways they were so bored."

"We tested them yesterday and they were all still virus-free. But we need to wait a little while longer. The incubation period can be up to twenty-one days, but it's often shorter."

"I know. I thought I'd stop by, take temperatures, and make sure everyone is still healthy before heading over for my duties."

Will stopped his stride. "I'd better do that. As time passes, two things can happen. Either a patient is healthy, or the risk that they'll get sick becomes greater. So far no one has done so, but we need to be as cautious as possible. Once I make a check, I'll see you in the hospital and let you know what I find."

Dillon didn't fight Will's logic, even though he wanted to see his friends. He worried about them and had spent quite a bit of time talking with each of them. Mostly it was listening as one by one they opened up. Each time it happened, Dillon felt like he'd won a small victory by gaining their trust. Will turned toward the quarantine area, and Dillon continued on to the hospital.

"Doctor," Mary said to him as he left one of the patient areas a few hours later. Dillon knew that wasn't her real name, but the one she went by for ease. "Dr. Scarlet wishes to see you." She motioned toward the ward exit.

"Thank you." Dillon made sure he'd updated the chart. "He should be ready to leave tomorrow."

"Good," Mary said, and Dillon left the ward, finding Will outside in the hallway, looking drawn and eyes wide.

"What's wrong? Is it the boys?" Dillon asked.

Will shook his head. "The mother and aunt. They both have fevers, and we're transporting them to the isolation ward. I'll start treatment right away, but it seems the fever started sometime in the night. Both of them are dehydrated and only partially conscious. We've started IVs and I'm hopeful at this point, but it means that we're segregating the three boys further. They were the last people to have contact. I'm hoping it wasn't close enough for transmission. The boys all say they followed the rules and kept their distance, but I don't know."

"God, so now they have to start the quarantine period over," Dillon said.

"Yes, and they've been potentially twice exposed. You're going to have to keep your distance as well. Either this or the earlier exposure could still result in transmission. The three of them are close enough that I'm afraid if one gets it, they all will."

"If you separate them, they'll have no one," Dillon said and felt slightly light-headed. These boys weren't merely patients, but friends of a sort. He'd gotten to know them.

"I know. They insist on staying together. All for one…." Will smiled slightly.

"Of course they do. Their worlds have come crashing down little by little and they're all they have left." Dillon so wanted to be able to see them, even though there wasn't anything he could really do. "What will happen if their mother and aunt die?"

"Hopefully someone in the village will be willing to take them in. They've lived with and known these people all their lives. That's one of the beautiful things about village life, or so I've come to understand. They take care of their own."

Dillon hoped like hell what Will said was true. "I better get back to work."

"I'll let you know if anything changes," Will told him. Dillon nodded, and they went their separate ways.

Dillon went back to work and forced his concentration on the task and patients at hand. He tried to give them his best effort, but his heart wasn't in it. His thoughts kept returning to those three young boys. In the afternoon, when he could take a break, he arranged to use the telephone to call home. Not that he was particularly looking forward to it, but he'd said he'd call.

"Hi, Mom," Dillon said when the call finally connected. He'd had to try a few times.

"Dillon, where are you? Are you all right? You're not sick, are you? We've been hearing the most dreadful things on the news. Your father and I watch it every night to see what's going on." She sounded frantic.

"I'm fine. Not sick, and I'm really helping here. I think I'm learning to be a team player, if you can believe that." He swallowed. "I called because I needed to talk to you. Do you have some time?"

She scoffed, a sound he had never heard his mother make before. "Of course I have time." He heard the phone shuffle. "James, it's Dillon. Pick up the other phone." That was a surprise. "What do you want to talk about?"

"Nothing in particular. I have some patients... well, not patients, young friends whose fathers have died and their last remaining parents have Ebola now. They could lose their entire families." Dillon swallowed as he heard his father come on the line.

"How are you, Dillon?" his father asked in his usual rather stiff tone.

"I'm fine, Dad. It's very different here, as you might expect." He kept his tone almost businesslike, the way his father seemed to prefer it.

"But you're holding up okay and doing well?" his father asked.

"Of course. Everything is fine. I just called to see how you were. I'm very busy and work long hours. It's like being a resident once again."

"Are you working with Ebola patients?"

"Not directly. But I'm working with people who supervise their care. One of the doctors has had the disease, so now he's immune. He works with the patients directly. He still has to be careful, but he can get closer than most of us."

"Why you had to go I'm sure I don't know, but do good work while you're there." Dillon heard the phone disconnect and shook his head. That had to be one of the strangest conversations he'd ever had with his father.

"He's been just as worried about you as I have," his mother said. Dillon simply shrugged it off. "So what do you want to talk about?"

"Nothing. The possibility of those boys losing their family made me want to talk with mine." He wasn't sure what he'd been expecting out of this conversation, exactly. He and his parents hadn't been close in a while, and the concern from them seemed to come out of left field.

"Well, I'm glad you called." She sounded confused. "Don't wait so long the next time. I worry that you're all right. Is there a number I can reach you at there?"

"Not really. The service here is spotty. It took me a couple tries to get through to you. I'll call again when I can. Try not to worry. I have friends here, and we look out for each other." Dillon paused. "I think this is turning out to be a very good experience."

"How so?"

Dillon had meant in the general sense and wasn't ready for her question. "I think I'm learning not to take so many things for granted." He fumbled over the words. "I can see my life much more clearly now." There was no way he could go into any details over the phone like this. "I need to go, but I'll call when I can, and you can write me." Dillon gave her the address. "Letters take a while, but if you write using the address I gave you, I will eventually get it." At least he hoped so. "You can also e-mail me. There is Internet and I check it when I can." He gave her the address to use. He wasn't really expecting much, but he passed the information on.

"Okay," she said. "Is there anything you want me to send you?"

Dillon laughed. "An air conditioner would be nice, and a generator and the fuel to go along with it. That would be totally awesome."

He heard nothing for a few seconds, and then his mother gasped. "There's no air-conditioning? How can you stand the heat?"

"You get used to it. There's a breeze most of the time, and it rains when it wants to. Mostly it's just hot. But the nights are sometimes very nice when the breeze is just right, and the stars shine overhead like nothing I've seen at home."

"So you do like it?" she asked, voice tinged with fear.

"Yes, Mom, I like it. But don't worry, I'll be ready to go home when the time comes." He found he liked that his mother was worried. Dillon really hadn't expected it of her. That might have been harsh, but he couldn't ever remember her being worried. She'd always left that up to the nannies or his boarding schools.

"All right. I'll look forward to it. Maybe I can have a party for you when you get back and we can invite some nice young ladies to—"

"Mom, I know you don't want to hear this, but filling the house with your ladies isn't going to make me choose one. You know that. I'm gay and it's time you realized I'm not going to change." It was on the tip of his tongue to tell her about Will, but he didn't. He'd said enough for now. Dillon doubted she was ready to hear about a potential boyfriend. And Dillon wasn't quite sure what he and Will were anyway.

"I know...," she whispered from the other side of the world.

"Thank you, Mom. And as for the party, if you want to have one, then do so, but let's not plan anything until I get home. It's way too early." Dillon checked the time. "I need to go, but I'll call soon." Dillon said good-bye and hung up. He stared at the old rotary-style phone in shock. He definitely hadn't expected any sort of change in his mother. He'd always thought her incapable of change, and yet she sounded different. Dillon didn't want to read too much into it. Yes, he'd gotten another perspective on things in this place, so different from home. Maybe his absence had done something he otherwise could never have done for his mother.

"Is everything all right?" Will asked when Dillon stepped out of the office. "You look stunned."

"I was talking to my mother."

Will's eyes widened beautifully. "No wonder."

Dillon stepped closer and shook his head. "It wasn't like that. She's worried, and that's unexpected. Apparently she and Dad watch the news for any stories, and she was really pleased I called." Dillon smiled, then his mind changed gears. "Is there any news?"

"Not yet. So far the women are holding their own. That's all we can ask for. The boys seem to be doing the same.

"I have to see them," Dillon said firmly.

"It's good that you care about them, but aren't you letting yourself get too emotionally involved? They're good kids, I have no doubt of that. This disease has ripped apart whole families and communities. I've seen it more than once. I know you want to help, and that's commendable, but you're only going to be here for a few months. You can't get personally involved with each patient. I know you didn't back home or you wouldn't have been able to survive." There was no accusation or condemnation in Will's voice. That was the only reason Dillon didn't tear into him.

"You don't need to lecture me on professional distance and objectivity."

"I know I don't. And if you suit up, I'll let you in to see the boys."

Dillon thanked him. "Has anyone else inquired about their welfare? If something should happen to their mother and aunt, is there anyone who can care for them?"

"I don't know," Will said with more than a hint of pain in his voice. "Come on, let's get you ready. You look like you're about to go out of your mind." Will led him back to the quarantine area. At Will's insistence, Dillon suited up, finding he looked more like someone from outer space in his bright green suit than he did a person. Then he suited up as well and the two of them went inside.

Dillon walked down to the boys' room while Will spent some time with the other patients, saying hello and making sure they felt all right. Many diseases could be tested for, but Ebola was largely undetectable until the victim first developed a fever. It was frustrating as hell. "Hello," Dillon said.

"Dr. Dillon?" Kparsi said with a small smile.

"Yes. I have to wear this."

"We know," he said, looking at the other two. "Can we go outside?"

"I'm afraid not, boys. We need to make sure you aren't infected." God, he hated talking like this. Dillon stepped out of the room and grabbed a metal chair. He took it inside and sat down across from where the three boys sat on the edge of one of the beds, their eyes all filled with worry and fear. Dillon wanted to scream at how unfair it was. "Your mom and aunt are stable. That means they aren't getting worse."

Topka and Kparsi nodded. Wamah partially hid his face behind Kparsi as tears streaked his cheeks. Kparsi put his arm around his little brother to comfort him. He was the man of the family—at thirteen or fourteen. "When will we know?"

"About your mom, a day or so, I'd think. But you boys have a few weeks before we know."

"We don't have it," Kparsi said forcefully.

"Good, and I don't want you to get it either. I want you boys to be able to go back outside, and then we can play soccer again as soon as possible."

Wamah said something that Dillon didn't understand. He and Kparsi had a brief conversation that ended with Kparsi pulling his brother tighter. "He wanted to know if he could see Mama. I told him that we can't. Wamah doesn't speak much English. Maybe I will teach him while we're in here." This had to feel like prison for them. Dillon thought about what he could find to help them pass the time. He wasn't sure what there was, but he'd ask Will.

Topka stood, stomping toward the other bed. He turned toward Dillon, his arms folded over his chest. "I want to leave," he demanded.

"I know you do. But you can't. If you do, you could spread the disease to all your other friends." Dillon remembered the larger group of boys they'd played soccer with that first time. He tried to remember their names, but there had been so many. "We need to keep you safe, and I promise I'll be back as often as I can." He needed to leave or he was going to get too emotional.

"You don't have to," Topka challenged. "We'll all be good." Dillon paused at the choice of words. "We can look after ourselves."

"I know you can." Dillon stood and left it there. He didn't want to get into an argument. He also wasn't going to leave the three of them alone—that just wasn't going to happen. Dillon wished he could let them see him smile. He wanted to give them some sort of assurance, but there was nothing he could honestly say. "I'll try to find some things to help you pass the time." That was the best he could do at the moment. Dillon left the room and found Will leaving another room just down the hall.

"Everyone seems to be doing all right. They're bored," Will said.

"So are the boys, and they need something to help pass the time."

"Of course they do. They're used to being outside most of the time, and now they're cooped up in that room. Come on, let's see what we can do, for all of them." Will strode toward the exit, and once they were out, they stripped off the protective gear. Will then led him through the hospital to what looked like a supply closet. "We don't have a lot and never know when more will arrive." Will pulled open the door and turned on a light. The room was lined with shelves.

"Where did all this come from?"

"Missionary groups, schools, all over...." Will reached up to a shelf and pulled down a coloring book and crayons. He also got some colored paper and pencils. There were some games, and Dillon grabbed one along with a deck of cards and a checkerboard. It was a start. The boys would like all this. "I don't have a lot of other supplies, and what we have needs to last until more arrives. Patel is judicious, but I figure what good does it do anyone in here?" Will turned and smiled. "Grab something for the other kids and I'll take it in to them."

Dillon picked out a few more things and handed them to Will. Then they turned off the light and closed the door. He waited outside the area while Will quickly put on a gown, mask, and gloves and went in with his arms loaded. He came out empty-handed a few minutes later. When he took off his mask, he had a smile on his face.

"I take it that helped?" Dillon asked.

"They actually smiled when I handed them the things. I said you wanted them to have this, and they said to tell you thank you." Will gave him another smile. "Let's get back to work. I'm sure we both have things to do and I'm already tired."

Dillon knew how he felt. He lifted his coat from the peg and put it on before heading back to the regular wards to check on patients.

THE REST of the day wasn't just busy, but hyperpaced. Dillon never got a chance to sit down. He continued covering most of the patients in the nonisolation wards as others poured in, threatening to completely overwhelm them. The medical staff did its best, but more and more death chants sounded throughout the day and into the night. Every time it happened, Dillon hoped it wasn't for the boys' mother or aunt. When he saw Will later, Will told him they were still fighting. "The aunt is failing, though. I can see her getting weaker and I don't know how much more we can do for her."

"Topka is going to be devastated," Dillon said.

"I know. They all will. I need to get back." Will turned and hurried away, and Dillon did the same.

"Get some sleep," Dr. Patel said when he saw Dillon coming out of the wards well after midnight. "You aren't doing anyone any good if you get sick too."

"I will. I was going to check on the kids in quarantine."

"They're asleep. It's late, and you need rest. We all do. This isn't a battle you can win in a day. We'd been hoping we could head off this particular outbreak, but it was already waiting to bite us, so now we do what we can for the victims and try to prevent additional exposure. The government has already sealed off the area, so now we just wait and hope it doesn't kill too many people."

"How are our supplies?" Dillon asked.

"I've requested more and have been told they are on their way. But I doubt they'll get though because of the government blockades. So at least for now, we have to be careful with them."

"Is there anything more I can do?" Dillon asked.

"This is the hardest part about practicing medicine out here. Sometimes we need to make do with what we have. But regardless, no one is to take any unnecessary chances. We need everyone healthy and whole, so I repeat: go get some sleep." He flashed a worried smile, and Dillon nodded, already getting ready to leave.

By the time he got back to his quarters half an hour later, Dillon was dead on his feet. Will wasn't back yet. Dillon got undressed and cleaned up as best he could before falling onto his bed. He was asleep before he could think.

A warm hand stroked his back. Dillon thought he was dreaming. He had to be. But he rolled over and the hand stroked his chest. Dillon cracked his eyes open and saw Will looking back at him. "I was so tired," Dillon began, but Will silenced him with his lips. He slowly climbed into bed with Dillon, pressing against him. Dillon wrapped his arms around Will's bare torso, clinging to him. "I need…." God he wished he knew how to finish that sentence.

"Me too," Will croaked and then kissed him again—harder, more insistent. Dillon didn't stop to find out what had prompted this. All he knew was that Will was tearing at his remaining clothes and soon Dillon was naked and skin to skin with Will.

"Is it too much?" Dillon gasped.

"No," Will answered and crashed his lips onto his. This was the most intense Will had been thus far, but the need and desperation from Will ramped the energy and need for both of them. Dillon couldn't get enough of Will and clutched at him, grasping at his smooth back. God, he loved how this man felt in his arms—all lean, strong muscle, steel sheathed in softness. The duality was out of this world.

Will placed his forearm on Dillon's chest, holding him down as he scooted down. "Will?" Dillon gasped before wet heat descended around him and his initial cry choked into a gasp of delighted surprise. "God, I love when you do that…." Dillon gasped for breath as Will not just sucked him, but caressed his cock with his lips. It was amazingly erotic, and with each upward stroke, Will pulled Dillon closer and closer to release. When Dillon was nearing the precipice, Will stopped, leaving Dillon breathless. "Why?"

"I'm not ready yet. I want you to come with me."

Dillon's eyes were crossing, and yet he nodded as Will brought their lips together. He expected Will to drive him wild and then to fuck him into oblivion, but Will apparently had other ideas. He retrieved the lube and condoms, resting them on the mattress. Dillon started when the bottle rolled against him, and he retrieved it before it made a mess on the sheets. Will gently took the bottle from him and squeezed some on his fingers. When his fingers disappeared behind him, Dillon gasped. He so wanted to see those fingers as Will entered himself—how fucking sexy was that? After a few seconds, Will lifted his gaze toward the ceiling, inhaling sharply.

When Will was done, he reached for the condom wrapper, tore it open, and rolled the latex onto Dillon's cock. His sweet fingers felt so damn good Dillon nearly came. And when he straddled Dillon's hips and his body parted, allowing him inside, Dillon groaned long and loud as Will sank deeper and deeper onto him. God, the tight heat as he sank into Will's sheath was mind-blowing. The grip on his cock was almost too damned much. It took all his willpower not to thrust upward, but he knew Will needed time to adjust, so he remained still until Will lifted his body and lowered himself onto him once again.

"Damn, you're amazing." Dillon grunted.

"I like to think so," Will told him with a wry smile and plunged down onto him.

Dillon ran his fingertips down Will's chest, luring him closer before pulling him down into a kiss. It was sloppy, wet, and amazing, with Will tugging on Dillon's lips while Dillon pushed his hips upward, keeping his cock buried in Will's furnace of heat.

When they parted, Will lifted his head, gazing into Dillon's eyes, searching for something, but Dillon wasn't sure what. Then he moved again, eyes rolling back. Dillon drove upward, instinct and desire taking over, pushing him forward. It wasn't long before he'd reached the pinnacle of passion and tumbled over the edge, carrying Will right along with him.

Neither of them moved. Dillon didn't want this connection between them to end. But slowly Will lifted himself off, and they both moaned softly when their bodies separated. "I'll be right back," Will whispered and went to one of his drawers. He returned with a cloth and used it to clean them both up. Then Dillon made room for him.

Will lay down, but seemed tense.

"Do you want to talk about it?" Dillon asked.

"No… yes… hell, I don't know. There's nothing I can do about it. There was just a large number of people who didn't make it today. They arrived too late and were too sick for us to help." Will pressed his back to Dillon's chest, and Dillon wound his arm around him, slowly rubbing his smooth belly. "I know this comes with the job, but sometimes it sucks."

"I know," Dillon whispered. It seemed like they were in a constant battle with death and sometimes they didn't win. "I just wondered if there could be more to it than that."

Will slowly rolled over, and Dillon had to hold him so he stayed on the bed. "Is this just sex or is it something else?" Will asked. The question was a little out of the blue, but Dillon had been half expecting it.

"If I remember, you were the one who wasn't into relationships and wasn't sure what you wanted. I haven't exactly been sleeping around, and it isn't something I'm in the habit of doing." Dillon kept his tone level, but he was definitely hurt.

"God, I know that. But do you care about me?"

Dillon stroked Will's stubbly cheek. "Of course I care about you, and no, this isn't just about sex. I'm not into the whole 'sex without feeling anything' sort of thing. I like the whole package. Why?"

"We just never talked about it."

Dillon pulled Will closer. "That's because I didn't think you wanted to talk about it. The last time we did…." Dillon foundered for words. "I was trying to take things as they came, like you said you wanted."

"I didn't say that. I said I was crappy at relationships and that I didn't know what was going to happen."

"Will, you weren't exactly reassuring, so I assumed you wanted to take things easy and see what happened." Dillon sighed. "You know, we really need to say shit like this rather than assuming we understand each other."

"No kidding," Will said and grew quiet once again. "So you do like me."

"Yeah, I like you." God, this sounded like high school all over again. "Now go to sleep. The night's half over and we have to get up and save lives in a few hours." Will's eyes had already begun drifting closed. Dillon kissed him, and Will shifted over to his own bed. "I'll be happy once we have a bed wide enough for the two of us to share."

"I know. Me too." Will yawned, and his bed squeaked. Dillon turned out the soft light he'd left burning for Will all those hours ago and rolled onto his side. Fatigue, contentment, and happiness all combined, and he fell asleep within seconds. There was one thing about this place that was a sure fact: he worked hard enough that sleeping was never an issue. He only hoped the rest of the night would be quiet.

Chapter 7

THE FOLLOWING day was as frantic as Dillon had expected, maybe worse. But thankfully, toward the end things slowed down. Patients were all given beds, though unfortunately a few more died, but the inflow tapered off. By the time Dillon and Will got back to their beds, they could do little more than share a kiss before falling asleep. The next morning they were met at the hospital entrance by Dr. Patel. "You two check on your existing patients and then get out of here for the day. It's quiet for now, and you've been working yourselves to the bone."

"But there's a lot to do, and...," Dillon began, but Dr. Patel cut him off.

"I want you to get some relaxation and rest. I don't care what you do, but I want you two to take the day off. All of this will still be here when you get back, and the others can handle things. Tomorrow, another two will get a day."

"What about you?" Will asked.

"I'll take some time as well. The thing is, all of you need to be healthy and stay that way. So take a sanity day. You both need it."

Dillon looked at Will once Dr. Patel had turned and gone back into the hospital. "Is he trying to say we're crazy?"

"I think he's saying he doesn't want to go there. But...." Will looked around. "We are here in the middle of an Ebola outbreak, voluntarily. I think that could be the definition of crazy." Dillon rolled his eyes but didn't argue. "Come on, let's get our rounds done so we can go. I'll meet you out here in an hour."

"Okay," Dillon said, suddenly full of excitement and energy. He hurried inside and checked that all of his patients were progressing properly. He left notes on each chart for the other doctors, making double sure his intentions were clear. Then he met Will outside. "Is everything okay?"

"Yes. I checked on Kparsi's mother and aunt. They made it through the night." That didn't sound good at all. "We can only take it one small step at a time right now."

"Let's stop in and visit the boys," Dillon said.

Will nodded and they went to the quarantine area where they put on gowns, gloves, and masks before going inside. Dillon hated that he had to dress this way to see them, but it was better than not visiting at all.

"How are our mothers?" Kparsi asked.

"They're holding their own," Dillon told them. Kparsi translated for Wamah. Dillon had expected the three boys to have made a mess of their room by now, but it was as neat as a pin, with everything arranged precisely. They obviously took care of their things.

"Can we see them?" Topka asked once again crossing his arms over his chest the way he seemed to whenever they were there.

"Not yet," Will answered. "They are still very sick."

Topka glanced at Kparsi, who whispered something to Wamah, who went to the back of the room and sat down at a makeshift table with paper and crayons. "What are you not telling us?" Topka demanded in a low voice.

Dillon turned to Will. "They deserve the whole story."

Will nodded. "Your mothers aren't getting any better. For now they aren't getting worse either. We're doing all we can for them, but I don't know what is going to happen."

The two boys glanced at Wamah, who looked back at them. They weren't sure if Wamah heard them or, if he had, how much he understood. The thought of these three boys losing their family tore at Dillon. "We will let you know as soon as we know anything," Dillon promised. "And do all of you feel okay?" He'd grabbed thermometers and took each of their temperatures. They were all normal. He also listened to their hearts and took their pulses, which were a little rapid, but that was to be expected under the circumstances. "Take care of each other, and I'll be back to see you again later."

Dillon felt guilty as hell when it was time to leave. He wanted to stay and keep them company. Hell, he wanted to take each of them in his arms and comfort their fear as best he could. But he wasn't sure that would be welcome, and he knew he should limit direct contact.

"We will watch after Wamah," Kparsi said. Topka nodded, but that was all.

Dillon turned to leave, following Will out of the area. He sat on one of the benches to take off his gown and gloves. He threw them in the can with much more force than necessary, nearly knocking it over. "It's so unfair."

"I know, but we have to have hope that their mothers will recover."

Dillon turned to Will. "Look, we both know that as time goes by without improvement, the odds of recovery go down. This disease takes its toll, and if people don't respond to treatment early, it gets a stronger and stronger hold. So I know you were trying to keep the boys' spirits up, but you don't need to sugarcoat the news for me." He wasn't sure if he should be angry or grateful.

"We don't know right now. And that's all I can tell you or them." Will finished removing his mask. Once everything was taken care of, they walked back to their room.

"I don't want to go anywhere. I think I need to stay here." Dillon rubbed the back of his neck nervously.

"You heard what Dr. Patel said, and I intend to take him up on that. We need some time away, a chance to breathe and get our heads cleared, and you're coming with me. I promise not to take you away for too long, and you can visit the boys again later this afternoon." Will grinned with mischief, and Dillon wondered what he had up his sleeve. Will pulled out a small bag and began throwing some things in it. Once he was done, he walked to the door. "Get some things together, including a bathing suit, and meet me out near the front gate in ten minutes." Will threw him a fake glare and then he was gone.

Dillon turned back to his small dresser and found one of the smallest bags he'd brought. He put in a change of clothes, a bathing suit, and a towel. He wasn't sure what else he'd need, but he threw in some sunblock, insect repellent, and a hat before heading out.

As he approached the front gate, or what had once been the gate of whatever the property had been before it was a hospital, Dillon saw there wasn't much left of it, really. It was more like a ruin of metal and brick, but as he approached, a car pulled up. It was definitely something that had seen better days, with dings and dents covering most of what was left of the body.

"Were you expecting a limo?" Will asked as he pulled to a stop and rolled down the window. "Put your stuff in back and get in."

Dillon wasn't sure he wanted to have anything to do with the thing, but he followed instructions because, well, it was Will, and he obviously knew more about the safety of this rust bucket than Dillon did. He walked to the passenger side and climbed in, the door screeching as he closed it. "Are you sure about this?"

"It's fine. This thing looks like a pile of shit, but she's got it where it counts. And this way, no one will look twice at us." Will put the car in gear, and they sped away from the hospital. The roads were hell for a while, but got a little smoother as they headed west.

"Where are we going?"

"Where do you think? The beach. You came all the way to Africa and you need to visit the water." Will slowed as the road got rougher again. They seemed to be skirting the city, which was fine with Dillon. He never wanted to enter that pandemonium of traffic again if he could help it. Of course, he'd need to go there to head home, but that was enough. Dillon liked cities, but that had been outright chaos. He could do without that.

"Have you been here before?"

"Of course. It's a great spot. A little out of the way, but I like it." Will sped up as they shifted from dirt to pavement, such as it was. As they rode with the air whipping through the interior of the car, Dillon began to catch the scent of water and salt on the air. He inhaled deeply. The air seemed cleaner and fresher here. As they traveled, the air became heavier with humidity, but he hardly cared.

It was warm with a fresh breeze, and if he closed his eyes, he imagined he could be on a Caribbean island. "There it is."

Dillon opened his eyes as Will pulled to a stop at the edge of a cliff. "Wow!" Dillon breathed as he looked out over water and sky that went on forever.

"Yeah," Will echoed. "Go on and get out, but don't get too close to the edge. It's about a hundred feet down to the water from here."

"How do we get down?"

"We'll drive further down the coast, but you had to see this." Will got out and walked with him closer to the edge. The waves crashed on the rocks below them, sending spray that the wind picked up and carried along to them. Salty droplets misted Dillon's skin as he looked down over the edge.

"This is awesome. It's like we're at the edge of the world."

"That's what people thought this was for a very long time. There's nothing out there for farther than the eye can see, so you can understand why, centuries ago, people thought there couldn't be anything else." They were completely alone, and Will slipped his arm around Dillon's waist. "I discovered this place after one of the men at the hospital told me how to get here a few months ago. I was asking how to get to a quiet beach and he gave me directions to where we're going, but I took a wrong turn and ended up here first."

Dillon leaned his head against Will's shoulder. "Some wrong turn." He chuckled slightly and took a deep breath, letting go of some of the concern and stress that had been building up for since he arrived.

"Yeah, I know." Will took Dillon's weight and supported him. "Sometimes you need to do something for yourself. I know we're here to do a job and to help, but it's easy to get completely lost in the job, and when that happens, no matter what you're doing, you get burned out. So I come here sometimes to recharge. There aren't crowds of people—just the rocks, water and wind."

"I know that in my head, but in my heart I keep worrying about...." He let his voice trail off. He needed a few hours where he wasn't thinking about Kparsi, Topka, and Wamah.

"Those boys have really gotten under your skin, haven't they?"

"Yeah," Dillon admitted. "I'm not one to usually let that happen. I have young patients all the time. But just look at them. I remember what it was like to be their age. I was worried about getting a new bike, not worrying about whether I was going to lose a second parent in as many weeks. That kicks me in the nuts every time I think about it." Dillon glanced to Will. "I came here and I thought I would do my job, learn what I could, and go home. I had no idea this place and the people here would affect me the way they have."

"How can it not?" Will panned his head, and Dillon followed his gaze. "Look around. This place is breathtaking."

Dillon chuckled. "I was thinking of...."

"I know what you were thinking. But look anyway. This is a place of extraordinary beauty—water, rocks, trees, the spray on the wind that's just enough to touch your face and then evaporate before the next wave hits. And a few hours away—hell, less really—people are dying of a disease that most people in the world could care less about because it's here and not on their doorstep."

Dillon stiffened, and Will held him a little tighter.

"Yes, there were those cases in the States a few months back that made the news and gave everyone a chance to scare everyone, but then it disappeared, and so did all the talk and interest."

"You were here. How do you know what happened? This isn't the most connected place on earth."

"No. But I know how things work. A sound bite today, dead tomorrow. Get everyone worked up, scared, but without a call for action or anything. The media keeps everyone stirred up, but no one knows why they're stirred up because tomorrow it'll change. Given that fact, it's not hard to figure out what happened. Now there are quarantines we need to go through because we worked here, but do we get extra help to try to wipe out the disease at the source? No. Because it's Africa, and doing that would be hard." Dillon smiled at Will's sudden imitation of an eight-year-old. "So yeah, these people carry on as best they can, and some of them die." He turned his gaze away from the water and shifted it to Dillon. "It would take someone made of stone not to be affected by that."

"So you're saying I'm human?"

"God...," Will breathed. "I'm saying you have a heart, Dillon. A huge heart that somehow got opened up by this place."

"I've always had a heart," Dillon said.

"Yeah, but it was guarded and only open in ways you could control." Will stared at him, and Dillon could see Will daring him to ague. "You're a great doctor—you'll do anything for your patients, and they love you for it. Every one of the people you work with at the hospital says so. But that's all controlled. These kids got beyond those controlled boundaries."

Dillon sighed. "So did you," he admitted.

"I know," Will quipped, flashing a brief smile. "I'm just that adorable." Dillon rolled his eyes and then gave up and rested his head on Will's shoulder. "It's okay. I fell for you too. Scared the crap out of me, but I did." Will turned away and looked back out to sea. "I don't know what it means or what we can do about it. Relationships aren't exactly nurtured by what I do. What we do."

"Tell me about it. One of my colleagues has already been married twice."

"Was the whole doctor thing too much for his first wife?"

Dillon shook his head and laughed. "No. Parker can't keep it in his pants. Women throw themselves at his dark hair and deep blue eyes," Dillon brushed a stray lock of hair out of Will's eyes. "Parker can't help playing catch. But I think he's met his match with Char. Last time I saw him look at another woman, Char threatened to rip his nuts off."

"Sounds like they're soulmates," Will said with a grin that faded as he moved a little closer. Dillon closed his eyes. The wind increased and spray bathed them in wetness that added a slightly salty tang to Will's lips. It lasted only a few seconds and then Will's rich flavor came through. They dueled and explored with their tongues for a few seconds before they split apart, both of them inhaling for breath.

"How about we head down to the beach?" Dillon asked. Will nodded and they headed back to the car.

A fine sheen of water and bits of salt spotted the car. They got in, and Dillon held on as Will started the engine and took off like an excited teenager. He zoomed back down the road, and

Dillon wondered if the car was going to survive the journey. "Good God," Dillon shouted.

"Come on," Will countered, speeding up. They raced down the road and after a few miles made a turn and began to descend. The water came in sight, much closer this time. Trees and the occasional tropical tangle passed in front of the view until they burst out into a clearing. Will stopped the car and then an entire ocean lay spread out in front of them. Will turned off the engine and opened his door. "Go ahead and change into your suit. I'm going to get things set up."

He raced around to the trunk, and Dillon wondered what he was up to. Still, he grabbed his bag from the backseat, kicked off his shoes, and changed out of his shorts and into a bathing suit. Then he slipped on a pair of flip-flops and got out of the car. Will leered and whistled at him. Dillon colored and wished he'd brought some of those floppy board shorts instead of the square cut. Will seemed to like it, though, so maybe it wasn't such a bad decision after all.

Will lifted an umbrella and blanket as well as a basket from the trunk and then slammed it closed. He trudged across the sand, and Dillon took the blanket, spreading it out. Will set down the old basket and put up the umbrella, spiking it into the sand.

"I brought some sunblock," Dillon volunteered and got sudden images of putting on lotion leading to something much more fun and intimate.

"Me too. It's very strong, and a sunburn would be very uncomfortable." Will leaped and grabbed Dillon around the waist. Dillon's legs went out from under him and he landed on the sand with Will on top of him. He wondered what the hell was going on until Will kissed him, and then he didn't care about anything other than Will's lips on his and the way Will's hot chest and legs felt against him. Fuck, within seconds Dillon had completely forgotten where they were and pushed his hips upward, cock straining like hell to get out of the suit.

Will backed away with a sheepish grin. "Sorry," he whispered as he looked up and down the deserted shore. "I guess we're safe, but...."

"I know." Dillon would think nothing of being with Will on the beach back home, but here, if they were caught, they could be attacked, arrested, or worse. He needed to remember that. Hell, they both had to keep that in mind, because Dillon found he didn't tend to think straight when Will was around.

Will lifted off him, and Dillon stood, brushed off the sand, and sat under the umbrella. He opened the sunscreen bottle and began to apply it. Will sat next to him and did the same. After a few minutes, Will stroked Dillon's back to apply the cream. Dillon closed his eyes and soaked in the attention.

"Did anyone hug you when you were growing up?" Will asked.

Dillon thought that a strange question, but had to think before he answered. "I don't really remember a lot of hugging in our house. The nannies were kind enough, but they weren't my parents, so they kept some distance, I suppose. My mom and dad were never demonstrative."

"So you weren't touched a great deal. That doesn't surprise me."

"Why?"

"You jump when I first touch you. Each time you give this small start like you aren't sure what I'm doing. It isn't much—" Will's voice softened and he continued stroking, sliding his hands around to Dillon's side and then down to his lower back. Dillon leaned forward and held still. "But it's there. Like you aren't sure what's happening."

"I never thought about it," Dillon whispered. "I guess I never really considered my upbringing strange." He turned around. "That's not quite true. I always knew my childhood was different, especially once I got into school, but I never thought...."

"I wasn't picking on you. I was just asking." Will leaned closer. "You know you have nothing to be worried about with me."

"I know." But Will had him thinking. What else had been missing from his youth? He'd known his mom and dad were wrapped up in their own lives—he'd spent much of his time on his own or in boarding schools.

"You're all still and quiet. That can be dangerous." Will slipped his hands away, and Dillon straightened up and went back to coating his shoulders and chest with lotion. Then he took his turn and rubbed lotion into Will's back, enjoying the play of skin and muscle beneath his palms.

"Just thinking."

"Sometimes you do too much of that. I didn't ask you that so you could question your whole childhood. No one gets a perfect one, and believe me, everyone is messed up in some way. My mom used to say that kids don't come with a manual and every parent does the best they can." Will shrugged, and Dillon slid his hand up to his shoulders and rested them there. "Most people would kill to grow up the way you did. So your parents were distant. I had more family than I knew what to do with."

"I think the last time my parents tried to show their love, it was a woman named...." Dillon thought back and tried to remember the name of the woman his folks had set him up with and he couldn't. "God. There have been so many. Each one wanting to be Mrs. Dr. McDowell. Of course it isn't their fault. Each one was nice enough, but my parents don't want to acknowledge who I am, so they continue blindly forward, and since they don't have to acknowledge that I'm gay, they're sure someday I'll meet the right girl and settle down."

"Bitter much?" Will asked. "Don't let it get to you. They want what they think is best, even if they go about it badly."

"You don't know my parents," Dillon said and got to his feet. "Let's not talk about this." He stepped into the sun and then raced toward the water. His toes crunched in the sand until the water rolled around his feet and legs. He turned in time to see Will racing behind him. He leaped to the side, and Will sailed past, splashing down into the waves. Dillon laughed when Will came up sputtering with a smile on his face.

"Are there sharks?" Dillon asked.

"Possibly. There could be jellyfish too. So be on the lookout."

Dillon began walking out of the water.

"I'm kidding. With waves like this, there aren't jellyfish, and as long as we don't go too far out, the sharks will stay away. So don't worry and just have fun. We shouldn't go too deep anyway, not with waves this size." Will dove into one and came out the other side. "Come on."

Dillon followed, and they played in the water for a while. It was cool and refreshing after the heat. When Dillon got out, he lay down on the blanket under the umbrella and let the warm breeze wash over him. It seemed like a few hours in paradise without a care in the world. The tension, worry, and stress melted like an ice-cream cone in this heat. For a little while, Dillon could imagine that the rest of the world had slipped away. At one point, he rolled over onto his belly, the breeze blowing over his back, closed his eyes, and dozed off, finally letting go of everything.

THE SUN had begun its westward descent when he and Will packed up the car. Dillon refused to let himself think about what he was going back to. The concerns would return, and they did as it got darker and they got closer to the hospital. Will pulled through the old gates and parked the car off to the side of the hospital. Dillon loaded up everything he could and carried it back to their room. Will took the empty basket inside, probably down to the kitchen, and by the time Dillon had their wet things hung up on the line behind their hut, Will joined him. "I'm going over to see how things are. Why don't you go on and see the boys? They're probably climbing the walls. And since there's no one in the yard and it'll be light enough for an hour, take them outside so they can run for a while."

Dillon changed and then strode over to the hospital complex. He dressed and entered the quarantine area. It was very quiet and Dillon wondered if something had happened. People were always talking, even in whispers, but it was nearly silent. He found the boys in their room. Topka stopped midpace when he saw him, and Kparsi stood. They all looked at him expectantly.

"I thought we'd go outside if you want. Bring the soccer ball."

Instantly all three were on their feet, and Dillon led them through the doors and outside. As soon as they felt dirt under their feet, the three of them began kicking the ball around, running and calling to each other. Dillon stood off to the side. It was good to see them active, even laughing, though overt signs of happiness were fleeting. Mostly the boys worked off excess energy that must have been building for days. Dillon let them play until almost all of the light had faded. Then the boys joined him and they went back inside.

"Why can't we go home?" Topka demanded. "We don't have anything."

"How do you know?" Dillon countered. "It takes a while before symptoms appear."

Wamah whined softly, and Dillon didn't need a translation to know he was asking to see his mother. That tone, scared and wanting, reached deep into Dillon's heart.

"Dr. Will went to check on your mothers, and he'll let us know how they are," Dillon explained. Once the boys were again settled in their room, Dillon left the area and met Will coming toward him. "How are they?"

Will shook his head. "Both women are alive, but they're losing the battle. Both are weaker than they were this morning, and though we keep giving them fluids, they don't seem to be responding any longer."

Dillon turned back toward the ward. "What do I tell the boys?"

"The truth—they are both alive and that we're doing all we can. I'm going back inside. I'll see you later tonight." Will flashed a worried half smile and then hurried away. Dillon got ready to go back into the quarantine area.

When he arrived at the boys' room, all three of them looked hopefully at Dillon. "Both your mothers are alive. We're doing all we can."

"Don't lie to us," Topka challenged. "There is more. I can see it."

"I'm not lying. That's all we know."

"You expect them to die," Topka said.

This was the one thing he hated about being a doctor. He knew that hope was important, and the thought of taking it away from these boys ripped at his heart. He wasn't going to lie, but he wasn't going to take away what little hope they might have. "They are fighting the disease, and as long as they do that then there's a chance."

Topka shook his head. Dillon so badly wanted to hug him. Instead, he took a small step back and put his hands behind his back to keep from reaching out to him, to all of them. "They die soon?" Topka said.

"I don't know," Dillon answered honestly. "Dr. Will is there with them right now. All any of us can do is hope and pray." He'd never been a religious man, but he wasn't sure how the boys had been raised. It certainly wouldn't hurt.

Topka nodded, and Kparsi pulled Wamah into his arms as the young boy began to sniffle. Kparsi comforted him while Topka continued to stare into Dillon. "You come tell us?"

"As soon as I know anything," Dillon said. Topka pulled himself a little taller and nodded. Then he turned back to the other two, and Dillon watched him sit next to them. He turned and left the room, changing out of the gear before washing up and heading over to the wards.

Mostly they were quiet. He checked in on a few of his more critical patients, who were all sleeping well and seemed to be progressing. That was good news. What wasn't so good was the stillness that permeated the hospital. Dillon got a chill up his spine, a zing that something was happening or about to happen. He wasn't a superstitious person, but he couldn't shake that feeling no matter how hard he tried. By the time he'd checked on the patients as well as getting an update from the nurses, he headed back to his room.

Will wasn't there. Not that Dillon expected him to be there, but he'd hoped. Part of him wanted to believe that was good news. But he knew different. The news would be the same whether he saw Will in half an hour or half a day. Dillon got undressed, turned out the light, and lay down on top of the bed, listening to the sounds of the night. They were so different from what he was used too. Animals called, strange insects buzzed and sometimes bounced against the screens, and even the wind in the trees sounded different without the rustle of the maple leaves outside his bedroom window.

Dillon eventually fell asleep, but woke as soon as he heard the door open. Will came inside, trying to be quiet. "Is there any news?" Dillon asked and got no answer right away. He heard Will getting ready for bed and then the telltale squeak of his mattress. "Will?"

"The boys' aunt...."

"Topka's mother," Dillon clarified.

"Yeah. Her name was Celia, I believe. She... didn't make it." Will's voice broke, and Dillon instantly sat up.

"Have you told them?"

"No. I stopped by their room but the three of them were asleep. I wasn't going to wake them to give them that kind of news. I can tell them in the morning. They can have a few more hours of peace before everything comes down around them."

Dillon flashed on this last thread of hope being cut and the boys adrift in the unknown. "What about Kparsi and Wamah's mother?"

"She's still alive, but I don't know for how long. Some patients respond well to treatment, but others…. These two did at first, but they've slipped steadily downhill. It's very frustrating."

"I know," Dillon agreed as his medical mind kicked into gear. "This is going to sound morbid, but it's a shame we can't do a postmortem to see if there are other factors at play."

"Yeah, I wish we could."

Dillon hummed his agreement as his thoughts shifted to the boys. "I suppose we need to concentrate on the living."

He jumped slightly when Will touched his arm, just like Will had said he usually did earlier in the day. Now that he was aware of it, he recognized it.

"Go to sleep. Tomorrow is going to be a very tough day, and I'm afraid to going to get harder as it goes on," Will said softly, and Dillon closed his eyes, holding Will's hand. Once again, he listened to the chirps, buzzes, and calls from outside, but now they seemed to have changed, deepening and lowering until they turned into a funeral dirge. He knew it was his imagination, but that was what Dillon heard until sleep claimed him for a short while.

LIGHT HAD just begun to shine in the windows and Dillon was wide-awake. He got up and of course woke Will at the same time. They got up without saying a word, dressed, and walked over to the hospital. They both showered quickly, and once they were dressed again, Dillon took a deep breath before preparing to speak to the boys. He hated the protective gear he had to wear when he visited. It put such a distance between him and the boys—distance he wished didn't have to be there. Fuck professionalism—these were kids and they were going to need and deserved some sort of emotional comfort, even if he needed to maintain a physical distance.

"Dr. Dillon?" Kparsi said when he opened the door to his knock. He pulled the door open further. Wamah was still asleep, curled on his side on the bed. Topka approached, and Dillon locked gazes with him.

"I'm sorry," Dillon said to him and saw the last bit of light in the boy's eyes fade away. The hope was gone. "She fought hard and I know that fight was for you."

He nodded and stepped back, turning away. Dillon watched as his shoulders raised and lowered a few times, but other than that small movement, there was no indication of his grief.

"Can I see her?" Topka asked.

"Yes. The staff is preparing her body for burial. I know tradition says for the family to wash the body, but that can spread the disease and...." Dillon trailed off and simply nodded. "I'll go with you if you like."

"What about...?" Kparsi asked.

"There's still hope" was all Dillon could come up with without falling to pieces. Tears welled as he looked Kparsi in the eyes. He had allowed himself to get too close to these three, but there was no turning back now. "Dr. Will went to see what he could do for her."

Topka put an arm around Kparsi's waist, and the two boys supported each other. There was definitely nothing good or encouraging in the news that Dillon had for them. "Thank you," Topka said stiffly.

"I wish.... Is there anything I can do?" Dillon felt helpless and he hated that more than anything. Being a doctor had many rewards, but helplessness in the face of death was most definitely not one of them.

"Thank you," Topka said with a shrug and stepped toward the door. Dillon stepped out and turned back toward the door in time to see it slowly close and click shut. Dillon swallowed hard and took a deep breath through his mask before leaving the area. There was nothing more he could do for them. He could do his best to try to make the boys comfortable, but anything more than that was outside the scope of his care. He wasn't their family and he wasn't part of their culture. He was just a guy they'd played soccer with a few times and who was nice to them.

Dillon dropped the protective gear into the biohazard container and sat on the nearby chair. After a few minutes Dr. Patel sat down next to him. "How did they take it?"

"Stoically," Dillon answered before turning to face him.

"They are the men in their families. They need to act like it."

"They're thirteen years old and still boys. They should be out playing soccer, running, having some fun, instead of worrying how they're going to survive."

"The world here is very different than the one we come from. This world is rough and cold regardless of the temperature outside. There aren't any safety nets, no child services to help find them a home. I've already put out the word in the village that these boys are going to need a home. I hope someone will step forward and agree to care for them. Usually it would be relatives, but I doubt they have many left. At least that's what I gathered from the elders."

"So what do we do?" Dillon held his head in his hands, and for the first time in a while, he reminded himself that he had seven more weeks and then he'd go home. Seven more weeks and he could leave all this behind and return to a life he knew and understood. He knew how to function there to make things happen and get what his patients needed. Here he didn't have that. He was like a boat without a rudder or sail, floating on an endless bobbing sea, unable to move anywhere other than where the current took him.

"First thing, don't get upset. There are things that can be done, and we'll do everything we can for those boys. But you must remember that next week or next month, there will be another set of boys or girls just like them who will need just as much care and help as they do. It doesn't end with them."

"That's what sucks," Dillon whispered. "I came here to make a difference, but that doesn't really seem possible. People still die and children are still orphaned."

"We do make a difference. I know it's sometimes hard to see, but we do. The rate of infection in this area has dropped dramatically. People better understand the disease and how it spreads. Sometimes it's two steps forward and one step back, but we are helping, and you're part of that. You work hard and you've helped a lot of people." Dr. Patel paused. "I've seen this before. Everyone hits the wall at some point when they realize that everything isn't how they expected it. The world is harder to influence than we think."

"Yeah."

"But look at it this way. You aren't trying to change the whole world, just a small part of it. That's all we're doing. Making a difference in this little piece of it, and believe it or not, you are part of that." Dr. Patel stood. "So I suggest you take five minutes to collect your thoughts and then get up and move on."

"I'm not sure I can," Dillon whispered.

"You have to. There are people counting on you, including those boys."

How could Dillon explain the sad looks, the way they'd closed their door to him? He wasn't part of this world and he didn't really belong here. He stared down at his shoes and sighed. Yes, people were counting on him, and he'd never let one of his patients down before. He didn't plan to start now. He'd make it through the next seven weeks, and then he could go home. He could do that. He stood up and nodded. "You're right. I have things I need to do." He left the area and went over to the main wards and got to work.

He thought about his patients and the tasks at hand for the rest of the morning. In the afternoon, he went with Dr. Patel to the village. He had been scheduled to take part in an immunization and education clinic, his first. When Dr. Patel had first told him, he'd been excited, but now his thoughts kept wandering back to the hospital and the three boys.

"Are you ready to go?" Dr. Patel asked when Dillon met him out front.

Dr. Patel drove a small van the half hour to one of the farthest villages that the hospital commonly helped. Dillon wasn't sure what he'd been expecting, but it wasn't a few cobbled-together houses around two rutted streets that looked impassable. Not that it mattered, because Dr. Patel seemed determined to get where he was going, even if Dillon was shaken to pieces. "Here we are," Dr. Patel announced when he pulled the van to a stop.

Dillon stared out the window. People had already begun to gather, some in brightly colored clothes and others in what Dillon thought looked like rags. There were mothers carrying sick kids and children running and playing around the people in line. "Oh my God."

"Yes. These people all need our help. So take a deep breath and let's go inside and get started." He opened his door, and Dillon did the same. Dr. Patel went around to the back of the van, opened it up, and pulled out sealed plastic cases. He handed two to Dillon and hefted two himself, then he slammed the door closed and locked it. "The contents are valuable" was all he said as he walked toward what appeared to be an open area with a grass thatched roof.

"Is that it?"

"Yes. It will have plenty of air and keep us dry if it rains."

Dillon followed, looking around. Under the roof a few tables and chairs had been set up. He and Dr. Patel each took one and got set up. Then people began to file in, each taking a seat and explaining why they were there. Dillon asked each person their name and a few questions about how old they were. He took temperatures and looked at throats, ears, eyes, and skin. He gave immunizations and antibiotics for infections. At one point, Dr. Patel contacted the hospital, and soon after, their version of an ambulance arrived. Will joined them and arranged the transport of some very sick little girls to the hospital. A third doctor arrived, so another table was set up, and all three doctors worked a few more hours.

For the longest time, the line of people didn't seem to go down. At one point, the sky opened up, pouring rain on everyone, but they stayed in line, under whatever shelter they had, until it was their turn. The ambulance returned from its run, but thankfully there were no others who needed it at the moment.

A woman and her child approached Dillon's table. She was dressed in neat clothes and must have been waiting her turn for hours.

"What's your name?" Dillon asked quietly. He was starting to lose his voice from talking so much.

"Call me Bebe," she said. "This is my son. He does nothing but cry, and I don't know what else to do."

Dillon held out his arms and she gently handed him the baby. He appeared about six months old. His little face was scrunched up and his eyes were closed. "Does he eat well?" Dillon asked and gently began to unwrap the infant.

"Yes, but then he cries and cries."

Dillon nodded as he looked over the beautiful caramel-skinned baby. "When he cries, does he pull his legs toward his body?"

She nodded. "All the time."

"And is he gassy and burpy all the time?" At that moment, the little one passed gas loudly. Dillon nodded. It appeared he had his answer. "Are you breastfeeding him?"

She shook her head this time. "I cannot."

"So he's getting formula and milk?"

"Yes. It is expensive, but yes. The grocer in town get it for us."

Dillon nodded. "Just a minute," he told her and left the area, heading back to the van. He unlocked it and climbed in the back. There were a few cases of baby formula, and Dillon moved them around until he found what he was looking for. He opened the box and pulled out two cans. Then he closed the back of the van and returned. "Try this. You should mix it with bottled or boiled water. I think your baby is having trouble with milk." Dillon got a small bottle and opened one of the cans. He mixed the powder with some bottled water and handed her the bottle. She gathered the boy in her arms and began to feed him. Dillon took one of the chairs and placed it nearby where she could sit quietly while he vaccinated a few kids and earned some tears and an attempted kick in the shins for his effort. Not that Dillon liked shots either.

"How is he?" Dillon asked when he noticed that the baby was asleep in her arms.

"He is happy and no crying."

"It's the lactose in the baby formula you were using. He can't have milk. If you use this kind, it should be much better." Dillon handed her the cans. "Tell the grocer to get you this. If you have problems, he can contact the hospital and they can help you as well." The baby was still asleep, and she passed him to Dillon, who held him for a few minutes, letting him sleep in his arms. He seemed so content, and when Dillon touched his hand, he wrapped his tiny fingers around one of Dillon's. "He seems happy now. Have you always had troubles with fussiness?"

"No. It started a few months ago."

"When you switched to formula?" Dillon asked, and she nodded. "At first it wasn't bad, but it got worse, especially as you tapered off breastfeeding."

"Yes."

"Well, I think he should be okay now. Just stay away from milk and give him the new formula." Dillon handed her back her son. The baby opened his eyes for a few seconds and then slept again. "Has he been vaccinated?" Dillon looked over at Dr. Patel for some help.

"Yes. He did it the last time. Thank you," she said and moved slowly away from the area. A woman approached with two youngsters—a boy and a girl. Dillon immunized both children after examining them. They seemed healthy and strong, which was good to see.

By the time the line had dwindled to nothing, the other two doctors looked as exhausted as Dillon felt. Well, he was tired yet totally stoked. It had been amazing seeing all these people turn out and realizing that they'd been able to help them. Dillon figured he would never forget holding that sleeping, contented baby after he'd been able to help. That was why he'd become a doctor. Dr. Patel sent the ambulance back to the hospital, and the three doctors loaded the van and rode back. Dillon barely noticed the potholes and teeth-rattling ruts on the drive back.

When they pulled in, Dr. Patel parked the van, and Will came out to help unload and restock the back of the van for the next clinic. Dillon was ready to call it a day, but as he and Will were talking about getting some dinner, one of the nurses approached and motioned to Will. He turned to Dillon, and a chill went up Dillon's spine. Will nodded, and the nurse stepped away.

"Kparsi's mother?"

"Yeah. She's still alive but isn't going to last much longer. They've moved her to a separate room, and I asked her to set it up so the boys could see her. They'll have to look through a partition, but…." Will's voice broke. "Go get them and meet me outside the isolation ward. The nurse is going to clear the hallway so the boys don't come in contact with anyone, but they need to see their mother one last time."

Dillon turned and hurried toward the quarantine rooms. He had no idea how much time he had. Dillon dressed and went inside and right down to the boys' room, knocking on the door. Kparsi opened it, and from his expression he was already expecting the worst. "Your mother is still alive, but we don't know for how long. Dr. Will has made arrangements for you to come over and see her." Dillon wished they'd been able to do the same thing for Topka's mother. "I brought masks, and all three of you need to put them on. Gloves too, as well as gowns." Dillon handed them over to Kparsi and watched as the three boys helped each other put them on. Then Dillon led the way through the empty hallways to the isolation ward. At the door he knocked and stepped back. Will opened the door in a full body suit.

"We've created a clean space for them." Will looked to the boys. "Please don't touch me or anything else if you can help it. We've cleaned the area as best we can and brought your mother to where you can see her."

"Can we hold her hand?" Kparsi asked.

"Unfortunately no. We don't want any of you to get sick."

Wamah whimpered and moved closer to Kparsi, holding him. Dillon motioned them inside, and Will closed the door behind them. He pointed toward a glass wall and Dillon motioned for the boys to move forward. He stayed back while they moved up and were able to see. Dillon stood behind them.

Martha lay on the bed, her chest rising and falling slightly. She was on oxygen and had IVs going into her arms. Wamah called out for her. Dillon didn't know the words he used, but the tone was unmistakable, as was the pain in his young voice. All three of them stared in silence for a long time. Topka was the first to turn away. He stepped back while the other two talked quietly.

"Does she have a chance?" Topka asked, sounding much older than his years.

Dillon shook his head and hated himself for doing it. Yes, he needed to be honest, but still he hated giving this message.

"Is that why you bring us?"

Dillon nodded. "We wanted you to have a chance to say good-bye." Dillon stopped himself from reaching out to him. "I wish we could have done this with your mother, and I'm truly sorry for that," he whispered. There was so much more he wanted to try to express but he couldn't seem to put it into words.

Topka nodded but didn't say anything. Instead he turned back to his cousins, who continued watching their mother. Tears ran down Wamah's ebony cheeks, creating glistening trails of wetness. Kparsi's eyes were filled, but that was as far as the tears got. Eventually both boys backed away and joined Topka. Dillon opened the door, and they all stepped outside, with the exception of Will, who stayed inside the area.

"You will tell us when…," Topka began, and Dillon nodded once. It wouldn't be long. He knew that.

"Yes, I will." Dillon could only answer honestly. There was no option to hide what the situation was. He led the boys out and back toward the quarantine area. Outside he instructed the boys how to remove their gowns and masks so that no contaminants got on their skin. Once everything was safely in a plastic bag, he made sure the boys washed their hands and told them that they should all take showers as well. Kparsi promised that he would see to it that they did right away. "Is there anything else I can do?"

Topka shook his head, and Dillon left the room. He waited in the area until he saw the boys head down toward the shower area. Then he left and decided it would be best if he did the same.

Half an hour later, after a thorough scrub with antibacterial soap, Dillon was dressed in clean clothes, with the others in the hamper to be laundered. Then he put on his coat and prepared for rounds.

Yes, it was late, and he wanted nothing more than to be able to go get some sleep, but there was work to do and patients who needed him. Besides, the thought of going back, lying on his bed, and thinking of those boys for hours was not at all appealing. He was a doctor, he helped people, but right now he felt as helpless as he ever had. He actually thought of finding a calendar so he could mark off the days until he got home and out of this emotional meat grinder.

By the time he finished checking on patients and made arrangements for two of them to go home the following day, he could barely keep his eyes open. He stopped by the kitchen and got one of the sandwiches they kept around because of the odd hours many of them worked.

Dillon ate standing up and then went to find Will or one of the other doctors. He met Will as he exited the isolation ward. He looked at him expectantly.

"She's holding on," Will said. "I don't know how, but she is. I'm scared to be hopeful at this point."

"Okay. Are you done?"

Will yawned. "Yeah. I need to take a shower and then I'll be back."

Dillon yawned as well and headed to the room. As soon as he was inside, Dillon put his things away and sat on the edge of his bed, which was where Will found him twenty minutes later.

"Are you okay?" Will asked.

"I don't know," Dillon answered automatically. "As long as I'm working, I'm busy and don't have time to think. But...."

"Your mind races when it's quiet."

"Yeah. Like that lady today with the colicky baby. Something as simple as different formula back home is no big deal, but here... I keep hoping she can find what she needs. What if she doesn't? Her baby will continue to suffer. And those boys. Topka's mother has died, and Wamah and Kparsi's is probably next."

"We lost three other people today," Will whispered.

Dillon nodded, but it barely registered. "I know others have died and will continue to do so, but...."

"Those kids have put a face on the disease that isn't fading like it usually does for you." Dillon nodded at Will's insight. "I'm sorry I didn't warn you about that, but I didn't think you'd believe me."

"What's so different over here than from back home? I deal with critically ill children and adults all the time. I get called in when other doctors are having difficulty with a diagnosis, so I often get the difficult cases and misdiagnoses, sometimes when they've had time to go downhill. There's nothing more worrying than a child looking up at you with little hope from her hospital bed. She's been poked and prodded, feels bad, and is getting weaker by the day."

Will sat down next to him. "I know that. But here there is a difference. You never played soccer or laughed with that little girl. You only saw her as a patient. Granted, you're very good with your patients—caring, gentle, and understanding. But you don't get involved with them. You did that here. You knew those boys before their parents came in as patients. They got under your skin long before they ended up here."

"What do I do?"

"You feel for them and help them. It's too late for professional emotional distance. They're going to be orphans. This has happened before, and we'll do all we can to find someone to take care of them. Historically, Topka and Kparsi are nearly men. A hundred years ago in western society, they would be thinking of marriage in a few years. I know they seem young, and they are, but they'll both be men soon and they'll look after Wamah."

"You make it sound so easy."

Will shook his head. "It's not easy. They'll both have to grow up fast. Kparsi and Wamah lost both parents in a matter of weeks, and their father was acting as a father for Topka too. They're not going to have it easy. But they'll survive. The village and tribal structure will see to that."

Dillon wasn't convinced, but Will knew more about it than he did. "I hope you're right."

Will took his hand. "I hope I'm right too. But there's only so much we can do. We're here to help the sick and stop the spread of disease. We aren't social workers and we can't build their society the way we think it ought to be run. That's not in our scope and it would be wrong. I know you want to help, and you are, but there are limits to what you can do." Will scooted closer. "That doesn't mean we shouldn't try or care, but it also means we all need to know our limits."

"Then how does anything happen?"

"In my *extensive* experience, things happen when they're meant to. You and I are outsiders. We can have only limited influence, and then we go home and they go on with their lives."

Dillon blinked and turned to Will. "Did anyone ever tell you that you should have been a minister? Because you have that preachy angle down pat." Dillon waited a few seconds before smiling.

"Actually my original major was divinity, but I quickly realized that I was way too devilish for that. The whole gay thing, but yeah, my friends used to say that I could give a sermon on a moment's notice." Will shrugged. "What can I say? It's a gift."

"If you say so," Dillon said flatly.

Will sighed. "Okay, I know I can run on at the mouth, but I was only trying to help."

"I know, and I got snippy. Sorry." Dillon closed his eyes and leaned against Will. "I'm used to being able to find the answer to problems, but there doesn't seem to be an answer to this one."

"There isn't always an answer, or sometimes it's one we don't like." Will raised an eyebrow. "This isn't a book or a television show. You know that. In the real world, people hurt, and life sometimes piles insult on top of injury." Will sighed again. "Just stop me. I can't seem to help myself with this preachy thing."

"Maybe there's a drug for that."

"Yeah, I don't think so." Will stood and began undressing. "I'm going to go to bed, because there is one sure thing about tomorrow: it's going to be just as busy and frantic as today."

Dillon was pretty sure tomorrow was going to be worse than today. There was still a chance—the boys had hope, no matter what. He'd seen it. As long as their mother was alive, there was hope. Dillon told himself that over and over. It might not have been practical, but he had to believe that for the boys' sakes.

After Will got into bed, Dillon undressed and lay on his bed. "Stop staring at the ceiling and try to go to sleep. I know it's hard, but you need your rest." Will took his hand, threading their fingers together. "I probably haven't been much help, with the whole preachy thing and all, but I have to say just one more thing. The reason you're worrying and want things to work out for these kids is because you have a good heart."

"Yeah, right." No one had ever told him that before. People thought he was a pain in the ass, demanding, and just plain obnoxious.

"I mean it. If you didn't care, you wouldn't feel this way." Will's bedsprings squeaked as he leaned over him, lightly touching Dillon's lips. Then Will moved closer, shifting onto Dillon's bed, holding him until exhaustion caught up with him.

Chapter 8

DILLON WOKE with a start and sat up in bed, listening for whatever had woken him. His mind felt clouded, as though he was expecting to hear something that wasn't there. Instead, there was something else: the sound of rain dripping off the eaves. If he closed his eyes, it sounded like a summer shower back home.

"What is it?" Will mumbled from next to him, patting his hand on the bed.

"Nothing." Dillon lay back down and closed his eyes. "I used to love the rain. I'd open my window and listen as it spattered the leaves of the maple outside and drip, drip off the eaves of the building, which seemed ancient at the time."

"There's nothing like the sounds of home," Will whispered in a raspy voice filled with sleep.

"That was in my room at school," Dillon confessed. "I don't have those kinds of memories from home, other than the wind, I suppose. It never stopped blowing, even on warm summer days. There was always wind off the lake." Dillon grew quiet, letting Will go back to sleep. He kept his eyes closed and just listened to the rain.

The damn squeak of Will's bed told him he'd moved, and then Will pressed to him in the darkness. Dillon clung to Will, kissing him, holding him so everything—this place, the people—didn't make him shatter into a million pieces. He knew that when he got up there would be difficult things to face, but he wasn't ready for that. Not yet. An hour of rapturous escape followed by sleep was on offer, and he took it.

"Just lie back," Will whispered, his breath flowing over Dillon's kiss-wet lips.

Will kissed him again, hard and demanding, thrusting his tongue, taking charge and giving at the same time. It was dark in the room and there was nothing to see, so Dillon kept his eyes closed, soaking in the smoothness of Will's hot skin against him, inhaling his rich scent, amplified by the sultry air. God, he wanted this to go on forever. He wanted what they had to continue, but he wasn't ready to ask Will for that and get his heart broken when they parted to go home. Will's life was on a different path from his, like two trails that shared the same track for a bit and then veered apart, one heading south, the other north. Will stroked his cheek, pulling Dillon out of his mental wanderings, centering him on the here and now.

Dillon arched his back, pushing his chest forward when Will closed his lips around one nipple, playing with the other with his fingers. "Yeah, tease them," Dillon mumbled, the tingles from his chest blazing a trail to his cock, which jutted out the top of his briefs. Dillon thrust his hips upward, catching a bit of sensation that sent a shudder racing through him. "I need...."

"I know... I do too," Will whispered in response.

Dillon didn't know what he wanted; all he knew was that there had to be something that could quell the chaos inside. He groaned as Will scraped his teeth over his sensitive skin, mashing his chest to Will's lips in an attempt to get more. Thank fuck, Will gave it to him, sucking harder before sliding downward. Will didn't seem to be in the mood to tease. He sucked at Dillon's belly button as he tugged his underwear down to his knees, and then Will sucked the head of Dillon's cock into his mouth, sliding his lips lower and lower as the air rushed from Dillon's lungs. God, that was heaven, and Will reached bottom, taking all of him, swallowing around him, tightening his grip, pulling on Dillon's skin with his lips. It was like Will was trying to pull Dillon's release out of his balls, and damn it all if it wasn't working. Dillon shuddered, trying like hell not to come like a teenager. "Jesus, Will."

"I know what you like," Will said in a deep rasp after pulling off, Dillon's cock knocking against his chest. "Just like...." Will licked right above his hips, and Dillon shivered and tried to move away, but Will held him tighter and licked some more. "That drives you crazy because it's not quite enough. Or I can do this...." In a flash, Will caught Dillon's wrist and pulled it upward, and then he sucked right at the base of his arm, sending quivers of confused excitement down Dillon's back. Dillon didn't know what to make of the sensation and once again tried to shift away, but Will held him still and increased the pressure, sending a throb through Dillon's head. "See, I know you, what you like, what makes you crazy."

"How?"

"I pay attention to the people I care about." Will lowered Dillon's arm. "I know what you think you need." The phrasing was off, but Dillon didn't have time to think about it because when Will sucked his cock again, his brain shut off and all he could think about were Will's lips around his dick and how to get more of everything. Dillon ran his fingers through Will's soft, floppy hair. He loved the way it went everywhere and sometimes fell into his eyes. He caressed it and then flattened his hands on Will's head, grinding his pelvis upward, fucking Will's mouth. Part of him said to take it easy, while his baser half urged him to thrust for the moon.

Will provided the answer when he backed away and gently stilled Dillon's hips.

"Jesus!" Dillon groaned in frustration.

"Cool your engines," Will teased. "There's no rush to the finish line." Will kissed away the growl that had been forming on Dillon's lips and held him tight. Dillon kept thrusting his hips, sliding his cock along Will's pelvis.

Will lifted himself away, and Dillon stifled a groan. It was obvious Will wanted to do things his way. So Dillon took a deep breath to cool down a little and waited for what Will had in mind.

"That's better," Will whispered, slowly stroking Dillon's chest. "I know you feel you need some kind of escape, but that isn't what you need right now. Fast and quick will only be unsatisfying." Will chuckled and then gently wrapped his fingers around Dillon's cock, swiping his thumb across the head. When Dillon quivered Will did it again, this time even more achingly slowly.

"You're trying to kill me."

"No. What I'm trying to do is make you happy," Will countered and tightened his grip. "What is it you really want right now? I can make you come, you know that. You're so close to the edge you can already feel the come boiling in your balls." Dillon groaned at Will's sexy words. Instantly he was closer to the edge than he'd ever been. "I can feel how close you are. You know that? Your cock throbs slightly when you think about it."

Dillon whimpered as Will held him tighter, but didn't thrust. He tried moving his hips, but Will just moved with him so the effect was nothing. Not a damn thing, except another groan. "I still think you're trying to kill me."

"No. I'm trying to drive you out of your mind."

"It's working," Dillon whispered in return, and Will kissed him.

"I'm glad. By the time I'm done, you are going to be so wrung out and your brain so fried, you'll sleep for hours." Will stroked him once and then released his cock altogether. Dillon stifled the groan trying to form. He was starting to sound needy and whiny even to his own ears, so he bit off the sound and wrapped his arms around Will's back, pulling him down to him. Maybe it was time that he took charge for a while. Dillon tugged down Will's shorts and chuckled as he shimmied to get them off.

Now they were chest to chest and cock to cock. God, that felt so good. Dillon stroked Will's back, holding him tighter as their kiss deepened. Dillon cradled Will's rough cheeks in his hands, guiding them into a kiss so deep it touched Dillon's soul. In that instant he knew what he wanted, and that was for this… with Will… to go on forever. He didn't know what Will wanted, but it sure as hell felt like part of him was more than interested.

"You're thinking again," Will chided and glided his hands down Dillon's side before tugging his legs upward. Dillon wrapped them around Will's waist, telling him silently, his lips otherwise engaged, just what he wanted. Thank God Will seemed to be an expert at understanding body language—not that Dillon left a great deal of room for interpretation.

Will prepared him and then slowly sank into him, driving away all thoughts except those that centered on Will and the extraordinary way he made him feel. With Will, Dillon felt alive, happy, and excited, even if they were just walking together or getting his teeth shaken out by a drive down a rough road. And when they were together, like right now, with Will buried inside him, making those small movements that sent heat and chills racing through him at the same damn time, Dillon had no idea which way to turn or what the hell to feel or concentrate on. Instead, his mind went into overdrive and then gave up and shut down, and he let Will play him like a fine instrument. Will locked his gaze on Dillon's, and for a second it was as if a whole world opened up. He could see inside Will's soul to the caring person inside. That flash of brilliance only lasted a moment, but it was enough to add to the excitement.

Dillon leaned forward, tugging Will down in a kiss that sent heat flowing through him and out into the already hot air. Not that he cared for an instant.

"Do you have any idea how good you feel?" Will asked.

"I bet as good as you," Dillon muttered and kissed Will again. "No one else ever felt like this. Do you think it's because of where we are?"

"I think it's because of *who* we are," Will told him and angled his cock in just the right way, sending Dillon into orbit. "Sex is always better when the person you're with is special."

"Am I… special to you?" Dillon asked and his eyes rolled toward the back of his head as Will stroked along that spot that took his breath away.

"You better believe it. There's nothing more wonderful than seeing you breathless and panting for me." Will puffed out his chest, straightening his back as he thrust and snapped his hips. Then Will withdrew completely, and Dillon held his breath, hoping like hell he wasn't going to stop. He didn't. He slowly entered Dillon once again, filling him, and then pulled away. Fucking hell, that was mind-blowing. The empty/full alternation continued until Dillon wondered if he could take any more. Then Will went deep, thrusting hard, sending quakes through him and the bed. Hell, it felt like the entire building moved around them. Not that he really cared. Will could shake the building down, leaving them open to the sky and rain, and all Dillon would see or feel was him.

Sweat beaded on Will's brow and chest, rolling down his skin. He glistened as the first light of morning lit the window. Damn, he was glorious in the low light.

"Yeah, don't you dare stop," Dillon growled.

"Not stopping until you're ready to scream for me. Then I'll kiss it away and have you begging me to come."

"I... don't... beg. I may plead—Jesus—but never beg." He gasped for breath and saw Will smile. Fuck, Dillon knew he was in real trouble and was seconds from begging when Will took pity on him. Dillon stroked himself while Will drove him to heights of passion, whispering softly in his ear until Dillon could take no more. His breath hitched and his body stiffened. Steadily, slowly, he balanced on desire's knife-edge until he tumbled over, holding Will to steady himself and keep from falling apart.

Seconds turned to minutes. Dillon floated happily with Will holding him. The rain was the first sound from the real world to pierce the bubble that surrounded them. Dillon kept his eyes closed, holding Will, wishing the rest of the world would stay away for just a little while longer.

Dillon was so relaxed he barely stirred when Will withdrew, and by the time Will got out of bed and returned to wipe him off, Dillon was half asleep. Will's bed creaked, and then Will leaned over, kissing him lightly. "You're an incredible man, Dillon." Will stroked his cheek, and Dillon reached up, taking his hand and holding it against his cheek.

"So are you," Dillon whispered. Eventually he fell asleep, still holding Will's hand.

DILLON WOKE to an empty room. He blinked awake and yawned widely. With a sigh, he got up and began getting dressed. He checked the time and realized he needed to hurry over to the hospital or he wouldn't be able to get his work done and have time to see the boys. He shaved in a hurry and yanked on his pants and shirt, making sure to shake out his shoes before pulling them on.

He went directly to the quarantine area. He put on his protective gear and went inside, heading straight to the boys' room. He stopped when he saw Will standing in the doorway. Even in the gear, he knew exactly who it was and why he was there. Dillon approached as the first cry of grief split the air. It went right to Dillon's heart. He picked up the pace and reached the doorway as Will stepped back, their gazes meeting for a brief second.

"When did it happen?" Topka asked them as Kparsi did his best to comfort Wamah, but he was having none of it. Wamah clutched at his brother, filling the room and corridor with his anguish.

Dillon hurried forward, but Will grabbed his arm, yanking him back. "Dillon, you can't," he whispered.

"I have to." Dillon whipped around and shot visual daggers at Will.

"No. You can't help anyone if you're directly exposed, least of all these boys," Will whispered emphatically.

Dillon stepped back and stood next to Will, seething with helplessness. There wasn't a goddamn thing he could do to help them as the last of their hope and childhoods were wrenched away from them. "Dammit, Will," Dillon swore under his breath. "You should have made sure I was here."

"I did what I had to do," Will responded before turning and walking away. Dillon followed him with his gaze and then turned back to the boys. All three of them were now huddled together, talking softly in a language Dillon didn't understand. None of them was paying the slightest attention to him. He turned and slowly walked down the hall. Will was waiting for him outside the quarantine area. "What has gotten into you?" Will demanded.

"Would it have been too much to ask to wait until I was there to tell them?"

"Why? You aren't their parent or their family. They have none. Their mother died late last night, and I had to tell them. You know that. Waiting around was just prolonging the pain." Will took a deep breath. "I needed to make sure they heard it from one of us instead of someone else. You know that."

Dillon did, but he wasn't ready to admit it. Instead, he yanked off his gown and mask before peeling off the gloves. "It didn't matter. I had been hoping to help cushion the blow somehow, let them know someone cared, but they—"

"They're boys who lost their mother, and you're a nice man who's been good to them, but you aren't their emotional rock. They have that already in each other." Will finished taking off his suit and began to wash up. Dillon did the same without looking at Will. Yes, what he'd said made sense, but Dillon wasn't ready for things to make sense or to be happy and content. All he could think about was those boys. He could almost feel the grief coming through the door in waves.

"Dammit. She wasn't supposed to die." Dillon leaned on the sink, looking at himself in the mirror. "There was supposed to be some sort of miracle that would allow her to recover and be able to care for those kids." He turned to Will. "That's what was supposed to fucking happen. Not this." He stared into the mirror. "Why can't we get one of those miracles like they do on television, just once?"

Will didn't answer.

"Why?" Dillon asked, watching Will in the mirror. "Forget it, don't answer." He turned around. "I know I'm being stupid, but just once I want to see something like that happen. Those boys certainly deserved it."

"Things don't work that way."

"No. Well, they should."

Will stared at him. Dillon could tell Will was wondering if he was serious. He wasn't—not completely, anyway. But he really did wish there had been a miracle.

"Come on, Dillon," Will said softly.

Dillon turned back to the sink and finished washing up. Then, once he was clean, he left the area and got his lab coat so he could see his other patients. "I'll see you later," Dillon told Will and left the area to get to work.

He knew Will was right, of course. Things didn't happen that way in the real world. People died and bad things happened. There wasn't someone to step in at the last minute and make things better.

Dillon stayed busy—butt-busting busy—for the entire day. He stopped to grab an occasional bite to eat and then went right back to work, thankful he couldn't hear the laments for the dead that he knew were going on. Before going back to his room, he stopped to see the boys, but they weren't up for company. Wamah simply sat quietly, staring at the walls, while Kparsi did his best to comfort him.

"What's going to happen to us?" Topka asked. "I know we will be here for a few more days and we need to bury my mom and aunt. But after that…." It was hard for Dillon to hear Topka's voice break. He was usually so stoic.

"I don't know," Dillon answered helplessly, and after a while, he said good-bye and walked home, feeling even worse than he had that morning. At least then they'd been crying and showing their grief; now it seemed like they were holding it inside.

When he pulled open the door, Will was waiting for him. He got up from the chair where he'd been sitting, and without a word, he wrapped his arms around Dillon.

"I'm so screwed. I've let all three of them in, and I can't stop thinking about them. What the hell do I do?"

"You're going to hate me, but you need to back away. I spoke with Dr. Patel, and Sanjay said that he had already been in touch with one of the village elders. One of the women, a survivor who lost her husband and child last year, has agreed to take all three boys."

Dillon rested his head on Will's shoulder, letting the tears come. "So they're not going to be alone."

"No. They'll have someone to care for them. Apparently, from what Sanjay said, they know her. She's an acquaintance of Kparsi and Wamah's mother. She already knows the boys and has stepped forward to help them."

Dillon closed his eyes, buried his face in Will's neck, and let go of the fear and grief he'd been carrying all day.

"Are you crying?" Will asked.

"Yes," Dillon mumbled. "I know it isn't manly, but I can't help it. That's such a relief."

"I told you that the village would take care of them. They'll live near where they did before and they'll have friends to support them. It's how village life works here. The boys have another week in isolation, and if they show no symptoms and their tests come back clean, then they can leave. Sanjay said that this woman will come in to see them tomorrow. Since she's a survivor, she's immune, so she'll be the best placement for them."

Dillon sighed. "It's funny, but I'm going to miss them."

"I think you'll still see them around."

"I don't think I should. I want to, but I don't know how good that's going to be for them… or for me. If I get too involved, then it's going to get more and more complicated when I leave."

"But you don't want them to think you don't like them."

Dillon shook his head and held Will tight. "At least they're going to be okay."

"Yes, they are," Will said as he stepped back. "Come on, you need to have something to eat because I bet you barely stopped all day, and then maybe we can take a walk and talk a little."

"I'd like that." Dillon hadn't even realized how wrapped up and stressed he'd gotten until some of it began to leach away. Then he was exhausted and wrung out.

"It's easy to lose your perspective. It happened to me on my first assignment. But I learned that you have to trust that we don't have all the answers." Dillon scoffed, and Will released him. "That was a terrible sound."

"Well, you seem to have a story for every occasion," Dillon said, lifting his head and wiping his eyes.

"I guess I do."

Dillon pointed at Will. "You just made the same sound." They both descended into peals of laughter. Dillon had no idea why, but he felt so in need of some merriment he went with it.

"Come on, I think you need to eat." Will opened the door, and they walked together over to the commissary for a dinner of sandwiches and soda. It was all they could find, but it didn't seem to matter. As far as Dillon was concerned, it was haute cuisine. He ate until he was stuffed; he hadn't realized how hungry he was.

"My mother would have a fit if she saw me," Dillon said, waving the sandwich in the air.

"Why?"

"My mother has definite ideas about what each meal should be, and sandwiches with white bread and lunch meat do not constitute dinner. And she would never have allowed soda. Junk food of any kind was not allowed in the house. I used to sneak in bags of Cheetos once I was able to drive. The nannies figured out they could bribe me with special treats to behave if they needed to." He took another bite and set the sandwich on the paper plate. "My life was so... bizarre compared to everyone else's." Dillon thought about the time difference and made a note to call his mother again.

"How often do you talk to your parents?"

"I've only talked to them once since I got here. I actually think my mother misses me. My dad probably hardly knows I'm gone." Dillon shook his head and ate the last bite of sandwich. "I think I've had enough."

"Me too." Will stood and threw away the debris of their meal while Dillon made sure everything was cleaned up, and then they left the small eating area. "Is there anything you need to check on?" Dillon shook his head. "Then let's go."

Dillon walked next to Will. He wanted to take his hand, but he knew it wouldn't be good if they were seen. Part of their ability to do their job was the trust and acceptance of the people they helped. Outside, they took a turn to the left and began walking. A breeze came up, rustling in the trees around them. "I like the quiet," Dillon whispered, glancing up at the stars. "Back home it's a different kind of quiet."

"Yeah, I know. There's always background noise from the city. But here there's so little of that." Will stopped, and Dillon did the same. He followed Will's gaze upward. "There are sounds from the hospital, but it's not the same. There are no cars and trucks or huge air-conditioning units."

"Well, I don't think I'd mind those too much," Dillon said. "It would help make some of our patients more comfortable if they weren't sick in this heat."

"Things are what they are," Will said philosophically.

Dillon didn't have anything to say to that. He knew it was true. They started walking once again. "Have you given any thought to where you'll go once your assignment's over?" Dillon had wanted to ask Will for a while, but he was afraid of the answer.

"I haven't given it any thought. I usually travel for a month or so and then return."

Dillon swallowed hard. "Have you thought about coming back with me? Our stints are up at nearly the same time. I have a house outside Milwaukee, and there's a room for you if you...." Dillon wasn't sure how to ask this. "We get along great, and after living together in one small room, the house will seem huge, but I wanted to ask you to come with me."

"To stay with you, like a guest?" Will asked.

Dillon shook his head. "To stay with me and see if there's anything more to... this?" He touched Will's hand. Granted, no one seemed to be around, but they were too close to home for a public display of affection. "That is, if you want to."

Will chuckled.

"I'm pouring my heart out, and you're laughing at me?" Dillon was seconds from anger.

"I'm not laughing at you." Will stepped closer. "You're cute when you're flustered."

"So you are laughing."

"No," Will said seriously, lowering his voice. "I think the offer is very sweet."

"But you're turning me down," Dillon filled in. Will didn't answer right away, and Dillon figured he was trying to find the words to let him down easy. "It's all right."

"No one has asked me to move in with them before." Will turned away and began walking once again. "I've spent my life going from place to place. It's my job to help these people."

"What about your own life and happiness? I know you love what you do. But you can do the same thing there. Granted, Milwaukee doesn't have the exotic ambiance we have here, but there are lots of people in need." Dillon had plenty of money—he'd help Will set up a clinic if that was what he wanted. "The hospital always needs great doctors, and...."

"You've given this a lot of thought, haven't you?"

"Yeah. I haven't said anything because I wasn't sure what you wanted. You don't have to come if you don't want to, or you could just stay for your break."

Will sighed. "I'd like that. But I need a chance to consider it. I honestly think it's time I made a change in my life, but I'm not sure what it is."

Dillon's stomach took a header and he went silent for a while. "I'd hoped some of that change might involve me. I guess I was wrong."

"You weren't. You're the one who made me start thinking I needed to do something different." Will stopped once again. "I like you, Dillon—more than like you—but I can't put it into words, not yet. Sometimes when you say something you can't take it back, so you have to be sure, and right now I'm not too sure of anything."

"I understand," Dillon whispered.

"I don't think you do. I'm not saying no. I'm saying I need time to think." Will's voice broke. "If I decide to do something else, I need to come up with a direction for my life. And as much as I'd like to think that's you, I need more. God, not another person, but a clear direction. I have never had one before. I sort of fell into this and just kept doing it because it was easy."

"You call living in places like this easy?"

"It was easy because I didn't have to let anyone in my life. I stayed in one place for a while and then moved on to wherever I was needed. I never put down roots, and everything I own fits in a couple of suitcases." Will turned to him. "Your offer is one of the nicest things anyone has ever said in a long time."

"Then why aren't you saying yes?" Dillon asked.

"I want to. But…." Will paused. "You're away from home in a strange place. And I keep wondering if you're going to wake up and change your mind. Or if I'm going to wake up and this is all going to be a dream. So how about this? I'll say thank you for the offer and I'll hold on to it. I won't hold you to it, though, if you change your mind. Being away from everything you know can change your perspective. Is that okay?"

Dillon nodded. It was as close to a yes as he thought he was going to get. "Sure."

They started walking again, side by side, together, companions and maybe something more. Maybe Will was right and his entire perspective had been turned upside down. He also thought maybe that wasn't a bad thing. "I'm pretty certain I won't change my mind."

"We'll see," Will whispered.

Soft footsteps sounded off to their left. Dillon moved back and then began walking, slowly stepping out of the shadow of the building. He saw someone in the distance, but they appeared to be looking the other way. Will joined Dillon, and they picked up their pace until they were around the corner.

"I feel like I'm trying to sneak into my bedroom after curfew." Dillon laughed softly. He felt happy and wonderful. "So you're my boyfriend."

"Yeah," Will whispered. "It seems like it." Will bumped his shoulder, and Dillon bumped back. Sure, it was pretty high schoolish, but he didn't care. He'd take Will as his boyfriend. They continued walking and looking at the stars. A few times they stepped into the darkness to kiss or touch, and when they reached their room and the door closed, they demonstrated in a much more intimate way just what being boyfriends meant. Making love meant more than sex. To Dillon, they'd been making love for a long time, but tonight it felt like even more. The word had never been said, but for Dillon it wasn't necessary. Each tender touch and whispered endearment told him all he needed to know, and in the back of his mind, Dillon was already making plans for life back home.

Chapter 9

FOR THE next two days, Dillon was walking on clouds. "What's got you smiling?" Teta asked. Apparently she'd been watching him more closely than he realized. They hadn't talked a great deal, but today she'd approached him. "Every time I see you, you're happy. Have you found a girl?"

Dillon shook his head. "I have plenty to be happy about. The outbreak has died down and fewer people are coming into the hospital. That means they're healthier, I hope, and that we're all making a difference." Dillon had to come up with something, because he wasn't going to tell her he felt like a teenager with a first boyfriend. That wouldn't go over well.

"I hear those boys are going to be leaving soon. It's a shame what happened to their family."

Dillon looked up from the chart he was reading in preparation for seeing a patient who was making slower progress than he should.

"But a lot of us have seen what they seen," Teta continued.

Dillon set down the chart. "Way too many people." He'd yet to work directly with the isolation patients, but he had participated in weekly discussions and treatment briefings. "It breaks my heart to see it."

Teta leaned on the desk, which was little more than a Formica table that had been scrubbed within an inch of its life. "I've been places and I've seen parts of the world, and I know most folks out there"—she pointed, but didn't seem to be indicating anywhere special—"don't really care what happens here. Do you know that when you go home, you have to be in quarantine for three weeks? Everyone from here has to be, the US government just said so. They're afraid of us."

Dillon had heard that, but he couldn't argue with her. It was all driven by fear and ignorance.

"But you have a good heart and you give everything you've got. I heard how you visit those boys every day, and you have since they came here."

"They're good kids who have seen more grief that they ever should have." He'd decided that seeing the boys was important. They'd also been spending a lot of time with the woman who was going to look after them. The village had buried both their relatives, and Dillon had arranged for the boys to attend as long as they stayed away from everyone else.

"Yeah, but you made it so they could see their mama one last time. I know what you and Dr. Will did for them. We all do."

Dillon's throat constricted. "We did what anyone would do."

"You care about those boys," Teta told him in a matter-of-fact way. "Like I said, you have a good heart." She turned and moved away. Dillon watched her, thinking about what she'd said, and then he picked up the chart and saw what he'd been missing all along.

"That's it," Dillon said out loud.

"What, Doctor?" Teta asked.

"I think I figured it out." Dillon grinned and hurried through the ward to his little patient. He asked him a few questions and got the answers he expected. "Your mom got a new water pitcher?" The little boy nodded. "And it's got bright colors?" He nodded again, his eyes drifting closed once more.

"It's probably lead," Dillon said and asked Teta to bring what he needed. Dillon smiled at the boy and breathed a sigh of relief. "He's going to be okay." Teta nodded and hurried away, returning with the pills. Dillon woke the boy and got him to swallow the pill with some water. "He'll need to take these each day, and make sure his mother gets rid of that pitcher. It's probably poisoning the entire family." Unfortunately this was all too common.

"I will," Teta said.

Dillon updated the chart and after watching the boy for a few minutes, continued on to his next patient. Once he was done with his rounds and checking on treatment, he went to find Will and caught up with him outside the isolation ward.

"Don't come too close," Will said as he stripped off his protective suit and began spraying it down with bleach water.

"I understand the boys' quarantine is almost up," Dillon said.

"Yes. I ran blood tests on all of them and they're negative. They've also shown no signs of fever. So we're going to keep them a few more days, and then with luck, they'll be able to go to their new home." Will smiled and hung up his suit in its place to dry. "You know you shouldn't be in here, for your own safety."

"I know." Dillon took a step back. He'd gotten too close and stepped outside, letting the curtain fall back into place. Many areas of the hospital used simply heavy-duty, waterproof curtains and plastic to create temporary spaces. He waited for Will to come out.

"So what did you need?"

"Nothing," Dillon said. "I finished up and was wondering if you'd like to get some dinner or something."

Will sighed. "Yes, definitely. I need to shower and then I can meet you at the room."

"I'll stop by the kitchen and meet you there," Dillon said.

After getting two plates of sandwiches and bottles of juice, Dillon left the hospital and carried them to their room. Dillon set dinner on the small table and had gone to get the utensils when his head swam in small circles. It only lasted a few seconds. He figured he was tired and hadn't eaten enough. He felt a little better and finished getting dinner ready, but ended up sitting on the edge of his bed, holding his head in his hand.

"Will," he said when the door opened, "I think I might have a fever."

"Oh God," Will whispered.

"I'm feeling dizzy, and it just came on a few minutes ago. It hit me all of a sudden. I was fine when I was in the kitchen, but now...."

"Okay. I'm going to get a thermometer. I'll be right back. Don't step outside." Will hurried out, and Dillon lay back on the bed and closed his eyes to stop the room from spinning. He lay still, afraid to move, and didn't open his eyes when Will came back in. "I met Dr. Patel and told him what's happened. He's isolating all the patients you've seen in the last few days, but that's most of the hospital."

"I know. I was careful and never came in contact with any of the isolated patients, and none of those quarantined have it, so I don't understand." Dillon reached for the plastic wastebasket and lost the contents of his stomach. "God, what am I going to do?"

"Okay. We're going to take your temperature, and then I'm going to set up some fluids. I also want to test your blood and we'll go from there."

Dillon carefully lay back down. "Please turn out the lights," he whispered. He didn't move and heard Will leave once again. When Will came back, Dillon gingerly began to get up. "Are you going to take me to the hospital?"

"No. We agreed to treat you here for now. Dr. Patel doesn't want to expose you to anything until we know for sure. So lie back and keep your eyes closed. I have the things I need to set up an IV and take a sample of your blood."

Dillon hummed his agreement, afraid to move his head in case things started coming up once again. He jumped slightly when Will snapped on gloves and jumped again when he poked him for the sample. Then he groaned as Will inserted the IV into his arm and taped it down. Will gently covered Dillon with a light blanket.

"I want you to rest. That's the best thing for now. I'm going to get this sample tested right away." Will got up and left once again. Dillon didn't move. He was definitely uncomfortable, and he tried to go to sleep even though he was afraid to. He had to call his parents and could only imagine how well that was going to go. But he didn't want to move and lay as still as he could.

Will came back. "Granger is going to run the bloodwork for us as soon as he can. I brought you some water, and I need you to try to drink a little." Dillon sat up and drank from the bottle, then lay back down, wondering what was going to happen to him. "Rest, and we'll know more in the morning." Will turned off the last light, and Dillon did his best to let go and try to sleep.

He thought he might have heard Will eating the dinner he'd brought back, but he wasn't sure. Dillon definitely heard the squeak of Will's bed, and then everything was quiet. He must have fallen asleep, most likely from exhaustion. He ached something fierce and woke to be sick once in the night. There couldn't be anything left in his stomach by then. "Are you still awake?" Dillon asked into the darkness.

"Yes, I'm here. I got some cool water while you were sleeping." He placed a cloth on Dillon's forehead, and it felt so dang good. He sighed and closed his eyes.

"I have it, don't I? I've got Ebola and I spread it all over the hospital." Dillon wasn't sure what was worse—having a potentially fatal disease or giving it to others. "I should have been more careful."

"That's the insidious nature of this crap. It sometimes comes on like that with little warning. You followed all the protocols and rules, so it isn't likely that you spread it to anyone unless you came in direct contact with your patients, and you usually don't do that. It isn't as though you've been doing surgery." Will lightly stroked his arm. "Just relax. We're taking all the precautions necessary, and we'll watch everyone. For now just relax and try to get some rest."

Dillon noticed that there was little definitive information in what Will had said. "Have you got the results?"

"No. They're working on them now, but it takes forty-eight hours. He started them as soon as I brought over the sample. He did say he'll have a preliminary result in the afternoon, but not a definitive answer," Will told him. "Just relax and lie back down. I'm going to keep pumping fluids into you. I don't want to treat you aggressively until we know for sure, but I also don't want to be behind."

"Okay." Dillon lay back down and tried not to worry, but that was like trying to hold back the ocean with a kiddie shovel. Eventually he fell back to sleep.

Will cared for him for the rest of the night and into the day. He hardly left him for a second. Dillon dozed and got sick a few more times before his stomach began to settle. "Your fever is down," Will said.

"I'm a little hungry," Dillon told him, and Will inhaled deeply, blowing out the air.

"We need to wait for the results, but I don't think it's Ebola. You wouldn't be feeling better already."

"Maybe it's your expert care?" Dillon said with a smile.

"Come on. I'm going to help you get out of these sweaty clothes and into something fresh. Then I'll go get you a very light snack, and we'll see what happens." Will felt his forehead and then took his temperature again. "Just want to be sure. Yeah, it's definitely down." He sounded relieved. "I'll be right back."

Will left the room, and Dillon went to sleep. He knew one of the issues with Ebola was that its symptoms, especially early on, mimicked so many other conditions. Thankfully, he felt better and they might have overreacted. Dillon hoped that was true. He waited for Will to return, and when he did, he ate the toast and drank a small amount of juice before lying down and closing his eyes.

The food didn't stay down very long, though, and Dillon groaned as he rested back on the pillow. Will took his temperature and placed another cold cloth on his forehead. Feeling more comfortable, Dillon went to sleep.

"Sweetheart," Will said sometime later, lightly stroking his arm. "The initial results are negative. We think you have a bad case of the flu or something. We're going to keep giving you fluids until you can eat again, and I'm adding an antiviral to help you fight it." Will took out a syringe and injected the contents into the IV line. "We can't be sure, but we've had good luck with this drug with our Ebola patients, so either way, we're hoping for good results. The best thing for you is sleep. I'll be here if you need anything."

"But what about the other patients? You should be helping them." Dillon's throat was parched, and when he looked at the water bottle beside the bed, Will helped him take a drink. Will's touch was so gentle and caring. It was different from when they were together… making love. "You're an amazing doctor, you know."

"Hey, just relax. I've been relieved of duty for a few days to care for you. We all need you." Will sat down but didn't release his hand. "If you want the truth, you had me scared." Will's voice broke a little, and Dillon slowly opened his eyes. "You're always so energetic and a force with everyone you meet. You don't just help people—you're like a ray of hope for them. You don't see it, but I do. The sickest patient will muster a smile just because you walked in the room. And to see you like this...."

"I'm going to be all right. I have you for a doctor."

"Yeah, but... you scared me, okay? I don't have many people in my life and...." Will stopped. Dillon slowly sat up, thankful his dizziness seemed to have abated. "I...." Will slowly stood and walked toward the door.

"Will." Dillon raised his head and made sure the IV line wasn't bent. "I think I know how you feel."

"You do?"

"Yeah. You stayed with me all night and then told me you're scared something is going to happen to me. It doesn't take an idiot for me to get a pretty good idea of what you feel." Will looked relieved. "But that doesn't mean I'm going to let you off the hook and not say the words. I know it's hard and you haven't had much luck in that department... you think I have?" Dillon would have laughed, but he was too damned tired.

Will nodded and continued looking at him. Dillon stared back, and although Will opened his mouth, nothing came out. Instead he shifted uncomfortably from foot to foot, and Dillon closed his eyes again, opening them a few seconds later to Will still staring at him. Dillon waited expectantly, feeling like Will was seconds away from saying what he wanted him to. A soft knock on the door broke the moment, and Dillon closed his eyes, lying back.

"Are you feeling better?" Dr. Patel asked Dillon after Will opened the door.

"I'm tired, but the fever seems to be down and I feel better."

"Yes. Will and I spoke, and we don't believe you have Ebola. We're going to keep you here just in case, until the tests come back, but we have a lot of people who will breathe more freely in a day or so." He didn't step inside. "Just rest and let us know if you need anything." Sanjay looked at Will. "Though I think you have everything you need already." Dillon wasn't sure of if Sanjay winked or not before he left.

Dillon closed his eyes and rested. When he woke, Will was there with some more juice and toast. This time Dillon kept it down, and he was pretty sure he was on the road to recovery. He also had more energy and shooed Will out to get some dinner. As soon as the door closed, Dillon thought about what Will had said… and what he hadn't. He'd been telling the truth: he was pretty sure Will loved him, because he'd fallen in love with Will. Hell, that was why he'd invited him to come home with him, after all. He still wondered what was holding Will back. It was a simple declaration of how he felt. Or maybe Dillon had been reading things all wrong and Will staying with him while he was sick had been just his medical training and empathy kicking in. Maybe he should have opened up to Will and told him how he felt, but Will seemed so reluctant to talk that he'd gotten cold feet as well.

There was nothing he could do except wonder, and in the end he turned off the small light and tried to rest. Sleep came blessedly quickly.

"YOU'RE GOING to be fine," Will told him the following afternoon. "As we've come to suspect, it wasn't Ebola, and the hospital has been taken off alert." He sounded relieved. "Your fever is down and it seems your appetite has returned as well." Will had removed the IV earlier in the day, but left the port in his arm in case it was needed again. Now Will removed the IV port and bandaged the small wound.

"Thanks," Dillon said with a smile. "Did Dr. Patel say when I can return to work?"

"Give it a few more days. You need to be back to full strength, so take it easy."

Dillon hummed his agreement. "What else has been going on?"

"Let's see, now that we know you didn't have Ebola, your patients are relieved, and thankfully none of them have come down with what you had. The little boy with lead poisoning is doing much better."

"What about the boys?" Dillon asked.

"Topka, Kparsi, and Wamah left today. They said to tell you good-bye, and when you get better they said they wanted to get together a game of soccer with you."

"How are they really?"

"Still in shock, if you ask me. Too much has changed for anything else. But they're with someone who has been through the same shock, and she seems like a very caring person who, I suspect, is missing her family just as badly as those boys are missing theirs."

Dillon sat up and adjusted his pillows so he was more comfortable.

"Teta apparently knows her and told me she thinks they'll all help each other," Will continued. "She also said she lives nearby and will help keep an eye on the boys."

Dillon breathed a sigh of relief. "Thank God they're going to be all right." He would miss them, but all he wanted was the chance for those boys to have some sort of life with someone who would care for them. "They've been through more trauma than anyone their age should ever have to endure." He held out his hand, and Will came over, sliding his fingers in between his.

"I know you're happy for them."

"I am and I'm not," Dillon said honestly. "I wish I knew they were going to be happy and I'm worried about them. What if someone decides to try to take advantage…?"

"Do you think Topka is going to let anything happen to Kparsi or Wamah? I think they're going to have to go through that boy to get to any of them. He's smart and he's tough."

Dillon nodded slowly, thankful the room stayed still. "That's true," he grudgingly admitted. "I guess I need to have faith."

"There's nothing else you can do in the long term. While you're here and when you're feeling better you can see them, but…."

"I know. I'm not their parent." Dillon had finally been able to put an idea around what he'd been feeling for them: protective, caring, wanting to shelter them. In other words, parental. But that wasn't what he was. He'd gotten himself all turned around. He had lost his objectivity where they were concerned and he needed to get it back.

"Exactly. But you can be their friend. Topka and Kparsi are going to have to grow up very quickly. Hopefully Wamah will be able to enjoy some of his childhood yet."

Dillon closed his eyes and ended up blinking away the tears that threatened. It wasn't fair. Not in the least. His childhood had been... well, different, with distant parents, but he'd never wanted for anything. Dillon knew the boys would most likely always be trying to make the best of what life threw at them. "Yeah," he agreed with a sigh. He couldn't help wishing there were more resources available to them.

"This is the only world they know. They understand it and it's familiar," Will told him as though he could read his mind. "They're going to be fine, and you need to concentrate on getting better so you can return to work."

Dillon agreed with that. He was sick of lying around doing nothing. There was nothing to occupy his time and he was going a little stir-crazy. Will was getting ready to leave once again, but Dillon stopped him, patting the edge of his bed. Will walked over and sat down. "Look, I've had plenty of time to think over the past few days. Lord, that seems like all I've had, and I want to tell you something."

Will stiffened as Dillon moved closer and sat on the edge of the bed. "You've been my companion here and, well, more than I ever expected to find. You helped me settle in and have guided me through some pitfalls and my own silliness."

"You weren't silly. You just got caught up," Will said.

"Whatever it was, I wanted to tell you that I've fallen in love with you." Dillon had let everything he'd been feeling bounce around in his mind and he'd realized that as much as he wanted to hear the words from Will, maybe he had to be the one to say it first.

"You scared me so damn much, you know that?" Will said. "We all rushed to a diagnosis because it was the most obvious solution, and out of fear for our patients and each other, but I was scared, and it made me realize that what I was holding on to wasn't as important." Will took Dillon's hand. "I know what I went through when I had Ebola, and it isn't pretty. Treatments have improved since then, but strong people still die and it's a hard fight. I didn't...

I hoped like hell you wouldn't have to go through that." Will swallowed hard.

"I'm sorry I scared you. Did you figure out what I had?"

"One of the local fevers. They come through here like influenza back home. Mostly the kids get them, since the surviving adults are immune. You probably contracted it from one of your young patients." Will took a deep breath. "We got off the subject." He chuckled softly. "Sometimes your mind skips all over the place."

"I know. I tell you that I love you and seconds later I'm asking about jungle fevers."

"Look, let me just say this." Will squeezed his hand. "You know we've got to be the most romantic couple on earth right now. Sitting here, alone, it's quiet, and we're talking about fevers and disease instead of what's really important."

"We're doctors. It's in our nature to be fascinated with fevers and disease. In fact, I think I'm beginning to feel a little warm."

Will placed his hand on Dillon's forehead. Dillon rolled his eyes and leaned closer, resting his head on Will's shoulder. "Oh…," Will breathed.

"Did anyone ever tell you that sometimes you're a little slow?"

"I am?"

"Sometimes," Dillon whispered. "You can be completely oblivious, but I think I like that about you."

"Why?" Will seemed truly perplexed.

"Because it shows that after all these years working in some of the hardest conditions possible and seeing things no person should, you're still naïve in a way. You don't look for ulterior motives all the time, and you take people as they come. That's really nice." Dillon wished he could kiss Will, but made do by gently touching the back of his hand to his lips.

Will shook his head and slowly turned to him, meeting Dillon's gaze. "You said yesterday that you already knew how I felt, so if you do, then why do I need to say it?"

"Because I said it," Dillon teased. "It would be bad manners for you not to," he added in a fake upper-crust accent that made Will laugh. "Seriously, if you care for someone, you tell them. It's part of taking the leap." Dillon scooted so he could see Will better.

Will nodded. "I do love you," he finally said. "But sometimes I wonder if I'm capable of knowing what love is. I thought I knew and that my mom loved me, but she turned her back on me. The others I thought I loved did the same thing. So true love, whatever it is, seems to be a mystery."

"Then it's one we'll solve together." Dillon closed his eyes and held Will's hand tighter. He leaned against his shoulder. "I'd kiss you but I don't want you to catch whatever I had, even though after all the time we've been together, you might have already."

"Maybe. If I do, then you can nurse me." Will slid his hand lightly around the back of Dillon's neck. It was rough from all the hand washing, but tender, and when Dillon lifted his head, Will pulled him close, pressing their lips together in a kiss that reinforced their words. "I do love you, Dillon. But I'm afraid as well. Being away from what's familiar, I just wonder if you aren't getting caught up."

"I know my own heart, Will, and what I feel. Sure, this is different, but it doesn't mean I don't know myself."

"Maybe," Will whispered. "But let me ask you something. At home, would you have gotten your feelings muddled about those boys?" Will hushed him with a finger. "I just made a point. I don't doubt how you feel, not really. I'm just a little scared because I know how I feel, and my heart isn't going to take another trampling."

"Then I'll do my best to handle it carefully. Does that mean you'll consider coming home with me?" Dillon smiled nervously.

"Yes. I think it's time I tried to make a home for myself, and I want to make one with you. You're a good man with a good heart." Will closed his eyes, like he was trying to find something in his brain. "Lord knows you stole mine."

"I think that's mutual," Dillon whispered and kissed Will again. "I want to keep you here all day to make love and—"

"You need to rest," Will said quickly. "And I need to get to work before I take you up on that offer." He kissed Dillon again, pressing him back onto the bed. "I know you think this is sexy, but it's the only way I can think of to get you to lie down." Will kissed him hard and then backed away, grinning like the mean person he was at Dillon's very visible excitement. "Sleep, get better, and tonight we can go for a walk." Will backed away, and Dillon groaned, instantly missing him. They'd expressed their love, and now Dillon was as needy as a teenager.

"Okay," he agreed petulantly. "I'm tired of being in here alone."

"You're being a doctor—you know we make the lousiest patients. So I'm giving you an order." Will lowered his chin and stared at him through his eyelashes. Dillon crossed his arms over his chest and said nothing. He knew that was what he had to do; he just didn't have to be happy about it. Will turned and left the room, closing the door behind him.

Dillon stared at the back of the plywood door and scooched down on the bed. Then he fluffed the pillow and took a drink of water before lying down and closing his eyes. Of course there was no way in hell he could sleep. Will had said he loved him. Dillon was too damned excited to sleep. Will had also agreed to go home with him. He'd have to arrange to call the lady who was watching his house and ask her to check that everything was clean and ready when he got home. Just a little less than six weeks and he'd return, with a boyfriend. Who in the hell would have thought that after spending years in the Peyton Place that was the hospital back home, he'd fly halfway around the world and meet the man who made his heart pound in his chest just from a look?

What the hell was he going to tell his mother and father? Not that it mattered. He'd given up worrying about what they thought. If being here had taught him anything, it was that he had to make the most of what he was given. Everyone here seemed to do that. Even three boys who had made the most of a soccer ball.

BY THE time Will brought him dinner later that evening, Dillon was climbing the walls. He'd stayed put, but he felt much better. He'd even spent time straightening things up and making sure everything was spotless in their room. Dillon knew he was bored stiff when cleaning sounded like a fun activity.

"Let me guess. Sandwiches," Dillon said, and Will shook his head.

"Pasta. It's got jarred sauce, but who cares. It smells great, and I'm so sick of sandwiches I could scream." Will set down the plates and bottles of water at the tiny table, and Dillon joined him.

Their knees knocked when they tried to sit at it together, so instead they ended up sitting on the edge of Will's bed, balancing their plates on their knees. Not that Dillon cared for a second. He was thrilled to be eating solid food again, and the scent of the spices in the sauce filled the room. He closed his eyes and for a second imagined he was at one of the Italian restaurants he loved so much back home.

"This is good," Dillon mumbled between bites.

"Slow down. You don't want to get sick again. You've just been cleared to return to work tomorrow—you don't want to be stuck here for a few more days because you got sick."

"God, no." That was enough incentive for him to put his now voracious appetite on simmer. "Thank goodness." He continued eating until there was nothing left on the plate. By that time, he was full, content, and his eyes felt heavy. He hadn't done all that much, but his full belly said to lie back and rest.

Dillon stayed where he was until Will finished, and then he gathered the dishes. Together they left the room and walked toward the kitchen. Will took in the dishes while Dillon waited outside in the warm evening air, a fresh breeze blowing in. He inhaled deeply and closed his eyes. If he was quiet, this could be paradise.

"You ready?" Will asked, and Dillon nodded. "You have to promise me you'll say something if you get tired. The fever can take a lot out of anyone."

"I promise, but I'm fine." Dillon said, and they began a slow walk around the compound. "I need to take some pictures of this place to show my parents. They aren't going to believe it. To them roughing it is eating domestic Brie." Dillon smiled as Will laughed at his joke.

"You said your family has money," Will commented.

"My parents are loaded. There's more money than they, I, or two more generations could spend. Dad, of course, concentrates on making more, and my mother has her charities and causes that she supports. It's all very respectable and about doing what will look good."

Will paused and looked down at himself. "Are you sure you're going to want me around? I don't know anything about society or mixers, cotillions, or whatever else it is your family does." The fear in Will's voice was palpable.

"Yes, I want you around. That's how my parents live, not me. I have a salary from the hospital and live on that. My parents have all the money in the world, but I somehow doubt either of them is really happy. They worry about what everyone thinks and how everything looks. Lord knows my mother would die before she spent time with the boys because some stupid friend of hers might think badly about the color of their skin or where they came from." Dillon stopped and stared up at the sky. "I used to dream of being away from them and on my own, traveling the world. Every year while I was still in boarding school, my parents took a two-week trip to Europe. When I was fourteen, they forgot to tell me they were going. I called her cell phone to ask them something, and my mother got angry because they were in Paris and it was the middle of the night. I remember being floored because I didn't know they were gone. Her response when I asked was, 'Well, we always go this time of year. You should have been able to figure it out.' Then she asked if it was an emergency, and when I said no, she said good-bye and told me to study hard."

"You're kidding."

"No. So I figured out what I wanted to do and did it. What the hell do they matter?"

"But what if they don't like me or if they reject you?"

Dillon turned to him. "I see my mother and father a few times a month when we have dinner. The last time they tried to fix me up with a woman."

"I remember that," Will said with a slight chuckle.

"I'd like to think my mother's coming around. We've had a good conversation a couple of weeks ago, but I have no idea if it's permanent or just her reaction to what's on the news. I suppose only time will tell. But they don't have a huge impact on my life."

Will sighed. "That's a real shame. My family is pretty messed up, and yours doesn't seem to be interested." Will's observation was spot-on.

"I know. It's pathetic of all of us, myself included. They refuse to accept me, so rather than make them see me, I go along and then bitch about them when they aren't there." Dillon took Will's hand for a second. "But that's going to change. I will not deny you or be ashamed of you. I also won't stand for fix-ups or the other things they've done."

"Fine, but promise me you won't walk away from them because of me. I could never live with that. Losing my family was too traumatic to put anyone else through that." Will released his hand, and they continued walking, Dillon looking up at the fluttering palms against the near blackness of the sky. "I know what that feels like, and once it's gone, you can't go back no matter how much you wish."

"What would you change? They rejected you because of who you are. Would you have hidden it from them? Married a woman to make your mom happy?" Dillon sounded snippy and backed off. He didn't mean it like that.

"No. But I keep thinking I could have tried to ease them into it. Maybe tried to help them understand before I sprang it on them."

"There isn't a good way to tell someone anything they don't want to hear or accept. I'm sorry about what happened, but it wasn't your fault. I know it's hard not to wonder. But you didn't do anything wrong." Dillon turned around and guided Will in the other direction.

"Where are we going?"

"I think this conversation is best had in private," Dillon said softly as they walked back to their room.

Once inside, Dillon took Will's hand and guided him to his bed, where they both sat down. "I know you went through a lot of trauma with your parents, but you are not going to be the cause of a rift between me and mine. They already know, though they sometimes choose to ignore it. I also don't hide. During the last fix-up, I actually said at the table that I was between boyfriends. I think my mom and dad wanted to choke me, but I was honest. I always have been. So…." Dillon paused and waited.

"But what about—" Will began and then stopped. "I don't know. I'm nervous okay? I didn't come from money and have never had much of it. I've worked for little pay to try to give back, and now I'm at loose ends." Will scooted back on the bed and leaned against the wall. "Everything is going to change. You have to give me a little time to adjust. If I ask questions, it isn't like I'm expecting you to have all the answers. I'm only giving voice to my concerns."

"Okay. I just want you to be comfortable with the decision you've made." He hoped like hell Will wasn't going to change his mind.

"I am." Will moved forward. "I don't want you to go through what I did."

"I know," Dillon whispered and moved closer, taking Will in his arms. "Everything is going to be fine. I actually think my mother is going to love you. After all, I'm bringing home a doctor." Dillon smiled, and he was pleased to see Will do the same. "In my estimation, that makes you a catch."

Will returned his embrace, still laughing. "I am, huh."

Dillon lifted his gaze, "You certainly are to me. An amazing catch." Dillon touched Will's chin, lifting it. "Never doubt it." Dillon kissed him, deepening it, the spices from dinner mixing with Will's usual rich taste. He explored Will's mouth and pressed him back on the bed. "I certainly don't."

Will embraced him and Dillon kissed him harder, amazed that this incredible man was in his arms and loved him.

"You need to take it easy," Will scolded, but there was no heat in his words and his eyes danced with excitement. Dillon slipped his hand under Will's shirt and slowly worked his thumb over a hardening nipple.

"Do you want me to stop?"

"No," Will said, his voice breaking. "But I don't want to wear you out."

Dillon kissed him again. "If I'm going to get worn out, I can't think of a better way to do it."

Will hissed softly when Dillon lightly pinched his nipple. "If you get sick again, I don't want to have to explain to Sanjay that it was because we had athletic sex and I completely wore you out. There are some conversations that should be avoided at all costs."

"Oh, please," Dillon responded, rolling his eyes. "I'm not going to break, and if you do talk to Sanjay, be sure to brag about your prowess. He might be impressed." Will's mouth hung open, and Dillon waited three whole seconds before bursting into laughter. "I think he has a pretty good idea what's happening between us."

"No way."

Dillon shrugged and met Will's disbelieving gaze. "I don't think he's particularly upset about it."

"Did he say something to you?"

"No. It was just a comment and a look he gave us. You completely missed it, but I don't think it matters." Dillon grinned. "You know, it could be the sounds coming from this particular room that gave us away. We mean to be quiet, but rarely succeed." Dillon pulled Will down into a kiss, figuring he'd teased him enough. "Does it really bother you?"

"No. I guess not. I was just a little surprised. I thought we'd done a good job of keeping things between us. You know how hospitals are."

"I doubt we have anything to worry about." Dillon did his best to kiss and touch away the remainder of Will's worries, which wasn't a difficult task. Within minutes, it seemed as though both of them had left behind their concerns in favor of reveling in their newly confessed feelings for each other. They had time and they took it, stripping away their clothes and exploring familiar bodies that seemed new and somehow different, hotter, more exciting through eyes and hands that now sensed something greater in each other.

"I think I'm starting to really look forward to leaving," Will whispered after sliding down Dillon's body, gaze glued to Dillon's, lips poised so close to Dillon's cock he could feel his breath on his hypersensitive skin. "I never do that because I really didn't have anything or anyone to look forward to."

Dillon opened his mouth to say something reassuring, but his words were garbled in the heat and excitement of Will's mouth sliding down his cock. Words weren't enough, and all Dillon did was gasp and watch as his cock slipped between the lips of the man he loved. Everything had more meaning and seemed deeper, more important. Each touch was magical, and within seconds, Dillon was breathless and out of control. He tried to warn Will, but his release came on him so fast that all he managed was to touch Will's head before he spilled himself down his throat.

He gasped for air, and lay unmoving on the bed, like a rag doll, happy and as contented as he could ever remember. He pulled Will to him and held him until he could breathe and had the energy to open his eyes. "Give me a minute," he whispered.

"It's okay. Your... enthusiasm pushed me over the edge too."

Dillon felt like crap for a moment, realizing that he hadn't even noticed. "I'll get something to clean us up."

"Don't move," Will said and got out of bed. Dillon didn't even have the energy to open his eyes and watch Will's bubble butt as he got the cloth.

Once they'd cleaned up, Dillon made room for Will. It was always a tight fit on one of the small beds, but Dillon didn't care. He'd share a postage stamp with Will if it meant being held like this.

"Go to sleep," Will whispered, lightly brushing the hair off his forehead.

"I'll do my best," Dillon responded with a yawn that said he wasn't going to have any trouble dropping off to sleep.

"I'm really starting to think that things could be wonderful. I can see us going to bed together, yours the last face I see before sleeping." Dillon opened his eyes to see Will's smile. "I really like the sound... and sight of that."

"Me too," Dillon agreed. He could already feel sleep catching up with him. Will held him for a while more, and then Dillon shifted to his own bed. "You know, we really need a double bed."

Will turned off the last light, plunging the room into darkness. "I was thinking a king with lots of pillows, some nice blankets, and an air conditioner that would turn the room into a refrigerator so you'd curl nice and close and stay that way all night."

"If that's the case, then why do we need the king?"

"Because you're my king and you deserve one," Will whispered. Dillon smiled and felt Will take his hand. That touch would work just fine for now. Dillon lay on his back, not moving, as his eyes slowly fell closed. God, it was nice to feel bone-deep happiness and contentment.

"You never know," Dillon breathed to himself.

"What?"

"Sorry, I was just thinking how you never know where you're going to find what makes you happy." Dillon smiled and Will hummed his agreement in the darkness, lightly squeezing his fingers. He was happy, but knew that phrase went both ways. He had no way of knowing what was around the corner, but disappointment and heartache also had a way of showing up when least expected as well.

Chapter 10

THE PAST week had been wonderful. Dillon worked hard, but every evening when it wasn't raining, he and Will took a walk together and had some time alone. They talked about everything. "I think I'd like to open a practice centered around children," Dillon confessed. "I like working at the hospital, but there's so much politics and people protecting their little fiefdoms. I've always liked working with kids, but it wasn't until I came here that things really became focused," Dillon told Will on one of their evening walks. "I know I do infectious diseases, but children have special problems that I think I can help with."

"I bet you'd be good at it," Will agreed. "I've thought about oncology. I've had so many patients over the years with cancer, but with the almost primitive facilities available, I haven't been able to do much for many of them other than surgery, some basic treatment, and a lot of prayer and hope. If I could do anything, I'd like to work to make more advanced treatments widely available. So many of the drugs that could help are way too expensive for most people."

"I agree with that," Dillon said as they continued walking. "You know, it really is quite beautiful here. Not what I was expecting." He stopped walking. "I don't know what I thought it would be like, but I wasn't expecting lush tropics. Maybe I thought it would be desert."

"What always surprises me are the people I meet. We like to think we're different somehow, but we're not. Everyone has the same hopes and dreams. They may take different forms, but people here want their children to have a life better than theirs, just like folks back home. They want their families to be safe and healthy."

Dillon understood that now. "I'll admit I didn't get that before I got there."

"No one does. It's something most of us have to see to comprehend. At home we have things pretty easy. We don't generally have to worry about the quality of our drinking water or where our next meal is going to come from. Children go to school— it isn't a luxury like it is here, and they're not expected to go to work to help support the family at twelve years old either." Tension filled Will's voice. "Sorry, that pisses me off. Kids should have a chance to be children."

"Yes, they should." Dillon patted Will's hand. "But a wise person told me once that we can't change everything. All we can do is make a small difference, and we do that by being here."

"Using my own words against me," Will said with a smile in his voice.

"Maybe, but you were right. We can't do everything, and saving the world is a pretty tall order. So we make our little piece of it better."

Voices sounded in the darkness, sounds of distress. It wasn't yelling, but there was definite tension. "Let's see what's going on," Will said, and they turned and headed out toward the gate.

"What's happening?" Will asked as he approached the small group of people. When they got close enough, Dillon saw Topka, Kparsi, and Wamah accompanied by a woman in a brightly colored and patterned dress.

"They no want us now," Topka said. He was trying to be strong, but Dillon heard the pain in his voice.

Dillon turned to the woman for an explanation.

"The village leaders will throw me out if I let them live with me," she said. "They say they bring disease to the village."

"They're all healthy. It makes no sense whatsoever," Dillon countered.

"Fear isn't rational," Will told him. "This isn't the first time. There have been a lot of children orphaned, and once they are, sometimes the villages don't want to take them because they think they carry Ebola even if they don't have symptoms. It's ridiculous, but there's always more than enough fear to go around."

"They say I will not be allowed to work if they are with me," the woman said. She went on to introduce herself as Juna. "I must work."

"Okay. It's going to be all right," Will said calmly, even as Dillon's temper rose. If what she said was true, then it wasn't her fault, but it still made him angry.

"No, it's not," Dillon interrupted.

Will flashed him a calm-down look. "Let's get all of you inside so we can figure out what we're going to do." He motioned toward the door, and they all walked inside. Will opened the door to one of the small consultation rooms, and everyone filed in. Wamah stayed close to Kparsi and looked completely heartbroken. These boys had already been through so much, and now this.

"I'll get Sanjay. Stay here with them," Will said and left the room. Dillon wasn't sure what in the hell to say. The boys, including stoic Topka, looked shell-shocked. It was completely disheartening. He had hoped the ordeal was over for them and that they would have a chance at some happiness.

Sanjay and Will joined them a few minutes later, and then Sanjay and Juna left the room, returning after a long while.

"What's going to happen?" Dillon asked as soon as they returned.

"The boys are going to spend the night in one of the empty rooms. We'll get some beds made up for them. It's too late to resolve this today, but we'll deal with this fully in the morning." He turned to the boys. "We will not leave you alone with no place to go. That isn't going to happen. We just need a little time to try to fix this." Sanjay turned to Dillon. "Take them down to the room next to yours. It's empty for now. It should be set up, and they can sleep there for now."

Dillon nodded and waited for the boys to join him. Each carried a small bag that probably contained everything they owned in the world. Dillon saw that Topka's was the largest, probably because he had the soccer ball. He led them outside and across the yard, then the door to the room. It was indeed set up, for the most part. Dillon got to work making up the beds and doing his best to make the boys comfortable. "We'll straighten this out," Dillon said, trying to reassure them.

The boys said nothing except a quiet thank-you once Dillon was done. Not knowing what else to do, he left after saying good night and telling them he'd see them in the morning. After leaving the room, Dillon took a deep breath and clenched his fists. That was so fucking unfair and ridiculous. It made him angry as hell. He stomped back to the hospital and into the small conference room. Juna had gone, but Will and Sanjay waited for him.

"Before you lose your temper, understand that Juna cares for those boys and wants to give them a home. There's little doubt about that."

"Then what do we do?"

"I don't know yet. They can stay here a few days, but not indefinitely. We aren't equipped to parent them."

"I know that, but my question still stands: What are we going to do? These kids need a home." He kept his hands under the table, clenching and unclenching his fists. This was pissing him off to no end.

"Like I said, Dillon, I don't know yet. Let me think about it tonight and we'll meet to talk over options in the morning. In the meantime you both need to get some rest. Check on the boys before you go to bed and do the same thing in the morning. We need to make sure they know we care. We don't want them to just walk away, which is a possibility, given the way they looked."

"Those boys have been through hell," Dillon said.

"All the more reason to take extra care that they know they're wanted." Sanjay paused and sighed. "I know what they've been through, and we have to find a way to help them. I'm just not sure what the answer is." He turned to Dillon. "When you see them, be sure to explain that we will help them any way we can."

"I will," Dillon agreed, but he wasn't happy with the answers he was getting. They had to do more than this. Sanjay stood up, and Dillon followed along with Will. He was still angry, but there wasn't a damn thing he could do right now. "I'll see you in the morning." He tried to keep the frustration out of his voice.

Dillon left, and Will caught up with him just outside. "He's trying to help," Will said.

"I know. I'm angry about the situation. This is so unfair. How could people just turn their back on these boys and Juna? She's doing a wonderful thing, and they're making her life difficult."

"It's fear and it's not rational." They walked across the yard and quietly knocked on the boys' door. Topka opened it and stared at them.

"Do we have to leave here too?" he asked, and Dillon's breath caught. This situation had even pierced Topka's tough outer shell.

"No. We came by to make sure you're okay."

Topka turned to the other two and then stepped outside and closed the door. "No. Wamah is hurting bad. He no longer talks much and stays with Kparsi all the time."

"Was he talking at Juna's when you were there?" Dillon asked.

Topka nodded. "He likes her. She is nice to him."

"We are going to try to help," Dillon explained.

"What you do? Change everyone's minds? They afraid of us." There was little emotion in Topka's voice, which concerned Dillon. He could understand fear or anger, but the lack of feeling had him worried.

"Juna cares for you and wants you with her."

"But she's afraid too."

"She's a survivor," Will said. "She's already had Ebola and can't get it again. She also can't give it to you, and since you don't have it, you can't give it to anyone else. So there is nothing for anyone to be afraid of."

"Tell them," Topka said, pointing, and then he went back inside.

Dillon turned to Will. "We have to do something."

"I agree." Will began walking toward their room, and they continued their conversation inside. "What do you suggest?"

Dillon was quiet, looking at Will. "I want to adopt the boys. I could get the paperwork done and they could go home with me, with us. I have more than enough resources to take care of them. And the house... well, I could sell it and get a bigger one."

Will stared at him like his cheese had just fallen off his cracker. "You're kidding, right?"

"Why would I be?" Dillon snapped. "They need a home, and I can provide one."

"That's… that's…." Will's lips continued working but he said nothing. "I think that's a little extreme at this point."

"Maybe."

"Dillon, they're children, not…."

"Not what?"

"You can't do something like that on the spur of the moment. That requires a lot of thought and preparation." Will began to pace in the tiny space available. "Are you always this impetuous? I mean, adopting three kids… have you thought about how they will adjust? Will they want to move to a completely different country… with two men they barely know?"

"I guess I hadn't thought that far ahead." Dillon's words had slipped out before he actually had a chance to listen to them in his mind. "But I take it you don't like the idea."

"I don't know if I like it or not. But what does what I want have to do with anything? You can do whatever you want." Will stopped moving and sat down on the edge of his bed. "I'm really tired, and there's going to be a lot of extra activity tomorrow, so I think we'd better just go to bed. It'll give you a chance to sleep on what you want to do." Will was angry about something, but Dillon couldn't figure out what. Yeah, he was probably being rash talking about adopting the three boys.

"It was just a thought," Dillon said softly.

"I know you want to help, but taking them away from everything and everyone they know…." Will's yawned and lay down on the bed. "Please turn out the light."

Dillon undressed switched off the light, then got into bed and stared up at the ceiling. He put his hand where he usually did near the edge of the bed, but Will didn't take it. Instead, Dillon heard the familiar squeak and then silence.

WHEN DILLON woke in the morning, Will was already gone. Dillon dressed and cleaned up before getting to work. He didn't see Will for much of the morning, and when he had a break, he stopped in to see the boys and even convinced them to start an impromptu game of soccer. At least the boys seemed to take to the activity. Wamah played, but Dillon noticed that he was very quiet, and after a while, the game broke up when Wamah went to sit in the shade of one of the trees and pulled his knees to his chest.

"I see you got them outside," Will said, startling him.

"Yeah. But there was no joy in it." His gaze settled on Wamah.

"Look, if you're serious about wanting to take them to the US with you and giving them a home, I'll help you."

"I thought you said it was a bad idea."

"What the hell do I know?" Will shrugged. "That is, if you were serious."

Dillon watched Topka and Kparsi kick the ball back and forth. "Part of me wants to take them away and give them things they don't even know they don't have."

"Is that why you're talking about doing this? To save the world? Because adopting these kids is so much more than that. It's being a parent, with school and day care and everything that goes along with it."

Dillon swallowed hard. "I hadn't thought of it that way," he admitted. "But it isn't as though I don't care for them."

"I never thought that for a second. But are you prepared for all that? I have to tell you I'm not. I've never given any thought to being a parent. Now that I have, I think I might want to have a kid someday. But…."

"I see," Dillon said and shifted his gaze back to the boys.

"There's no shame in rethinking what you want to do. There are other ways of helping them, and I think it shows a lot of heart that you would even consider it. But is it the most reasonable course of action for them… and for you?" Will's voice was so soft.

"I don't know what the hell I should do." Now that he'd opened his big mouth, he felt he should follow through on what he said.

"You were upset last night and said something in the heat of the moment. That doesn't mean that you should be held to it. I certainly am not going to tell anyone."

Dillon narrowed his eyes slightly, wondering what Will was getting at. It was obvious he wasn't hot on the idea of Dillon adopting the boys, and the more he thought about it, the less attractive the idea was. He really wasn't in any position to become a parent. But what had him wondering was the insinuation Will had made. "Are you saying... just for argument, that if I were to decide to adopt the boys, that you wouldn't...."

"I don't know. It's a huge responsibility, and I don't know if I'm ready for it. Are you?"

Dillon realized he didn't know, and that meant he couldn't be. "I guess not. I'd like to think...."

"Hey, it doesn't mean there's anything wrong with you. The boys need stability and the familiar."

Dillon turned away from the boys. "At least you were honest, and I need to be honest with myself."

Will smiled. "Then we need to do what we can for them."

"Any ideas?" Dillon asked.

"Yes. I think we need to go into the village and speak with the leaders. They can make a difference, and we have to try to explain. Sanjay thinks that's a good idea as well, and he's agreed to go in with us. He already knows some of the leaders, so hopefully he can help."

"Do you really think that will make a difference in how people feel?" Dillon asked.

"All the boys really need is a chance. People will see that no one is getting sick because of them, and the whole thing will be forgotten. The good thing is that Juna is a survivor so she can't give or get it, so the boys are extra safe with her. We have to try. Fighting superstition and fear can be a bitch. None of it is remotely rational."

"Okay. I agree. We have to give it our best shot. The boys deserve nothing less." Dillon shifted his gaze back to where Wamah sat under the tree, watching the other two. It broke his heart to see the pained look on his face. It wouldn't have surprised Dillon to see him break down into tears at any moment. "What do we tell them?"

"Nothing. We're going to leave in an hour, and Sanjay doesn't want to get their hopes up."

"I suppose." The boys needed hope, but they also didn't need them dashed once again. "I'll stay here with them and meet you out front in an hour."

Will left, and Dillon tried to get Wamah to play with them a little bit more. He had only limited success, but he was willing to take what he could get at this point. When it was almost time for him to leave, Dillon said good-bye and made the boys promise to stay in the compound.

"SO HOW do we go about this?" Dillon asked Sanjay as they rode the short distance to Juna's village. In Dillon's mind, he'd always imagined it as a small cluster of buildings, but it was actually a town of sorts. The streets were dirt and for right now they were dry, but after a rain, they'd be rutted mud. Vehicles of all kinds slowly made their way—trucks, a few cars, bicycles, wheelbarrows. It was a hub of activity. The buildings seemed cobbled together from whatever was available. Living was done out of doors, on porches or in chairs under trees. As Dillon thought about it, living outside, especially when it wasn't raining, probably made sense.

"I'm taking us to the mayor of sorts. He's the town leader, and at least in this case, he's also a tribal elder, so he will have some influence on how people think rather than just politically. If we can convince him, then maybe he can quell some of the unease."

"Does he know we're coming?"

"I sent word with one of the men who works at the hospital. It would be considered rude of us to show up unannounced." Sanjay pulled the old car up to a house that seemed a little nicer than some. It had been recently painted and roofed. The sun beat down on them as they got out of the car, and Dillon wiped the back of his neck. Sanjay approached the house, and Will touched Dillon's arm, stopping him. They stayed by the gate as Sanjay went up to the screen door and knocked.

A woman answered it, and Sanjay spoke to her. Dillon couldn't hear what was said, but she opened the door wider and Sanjay nodded to Dillon and Will. They stepped forward and followed her through the small, sparsely furnished home and then out back to a shaded courtyard.

"What can I do for you, Doctor?" asked a large man with a round face, perfect teeth, and huge, penetrating eyes. He was smiling, but there was power behind those eyes.

"Alex, this is Will and Dillon. They work with me at the hospital, and we are in need of your help," Sanjay said formally.

"You help the people here, so I help you," Alex said. His smile stayed in place, but his eyes remained hard and suspicious.

"Three boys lost the men and women in their family. They have no one. One of the women in the village has agreed to take them in," Sanjay began, and Alex nodded. He seemed aware, but didn't interrupt. "She had to bring the boys back to the hospital because the people who live around her have threatened her because of how the boys' family died."

"I am aware of the… situation. People here are afraid." There were other chairs, but Alex gave no indication for them to sit down. Dillon stood straight and tall, watching Alex closely. He'd spent plenty of time around men with power—perceived and real—and he knew their game.

"That may be, but Juna is a survivor. She cannot get or pass on Ebola to anyone."

"It is not her they are afraid of. Those boys have the disease in their family. They carry it with them."

"No, they don't," Dillon said sharply. "That's fear talking."

Alex's eyes widened. He was clearly not used to be spoken to like that.

"Ebola is a disease. It does not run in families. It's a virus, and you catch it from close contact with someone who is infected. Those boys were tested and quarantined for weeks while the rest of their family died."

"You don't understand life here," Alex said in a harsh tone. "You come here and then you go again. We live here."

"Yes, you do," Sanjay interrupted. "So do those boys, and they have lived in this village since they were born. I daresay you knew their families." It was clear from the way his eyes softened that Alex had. "As the leader of this village and of these people, it's your duty to help everyone. You have always been a good leader, strong and patient. You also listen to your people. That is why you are a leader. These young men are your people and they need your help."

A little flattery mixed with shame seemed to help. "How do I know these boys will not spread the fever? You are very quick to want to get rid of them."

"Right now they are living in the room next to mine," Dillon said. "I played soccer with them this morning. I'm not afraid to be around them at all."

"I see," Alex said.

"Sir," Dillon began and took a step forward. "There's plenty of fear around this disease. People are afraid, and I understand that. There's fear back home on the other side of the world. I understand how it feels to be afraid—we all do." Dillon made sure his tone was soft with a touch of firmness underneath. "But these boys need more than fear. They need a home and people to care for them. Juna is willing to do that, and you should be doing the same. These kids are your future, and they're hurting right now. They've lost their mothers. I'm asking you to put your fear aside and help them." He hoped short and sweet would work.

Alex's expression didn't change, and Dillon was sure that he'd blown whatever chance they'd had to get Alex to change his mind.

"Dillon has expressed an interest to me in taking the boys home with him, back to America," Will said. Sanjay appeared shocked, and Dillon's stomach fluttered as he wondered where Will was going with this.

"All three of them?" Alex asked, clearly surprised.

"Yes. He cares for the boys and feels very strongly that they need a home, so he's willing to help give them one. Would he do that if he thought there was anything to fear?"

"Then why didn't he say so?" Alex demanded, looking at Dillon.

"Because the boys should be with their family. This village is their family. It's what they know, and there are people who care about them. They have friends here. This is their world. Dr. Dillon could take them with him, but we are afraid that such a drastic change would make things more difficult for them." Will turned to Dillon, and his eyes were bright and forceful. "However, we would take them with us. They need a home, and we'll make sure they get one if that's what is necessary."

Dillon swallowed and hoped like hell that he kept the surprise off his face. Damn, Will was glorious just like he was at that moment—the righter of wrongs, a crusader of sorts. Dillon's throat constricted and he blinked a few times before pushing the feelings that welled to the side. Not that he didn't relish them, or the way Will looked at that moment and what Will's words truly meant, but he didn't want his emotions to show on his face.

"You'd take them with you? After what happened and how close they came to the fever? You'd take them with you anyway?"

"Yes, we would. If you won't care for them, then we'll have to."

Dillon watched as Alex looked at him and then at Will. He was clearly trying to figure something out. Dillon hardened his gaze and met Alex's, daring him to draw the conclusion.

"How do I know they don't carry the disease?" Alex asked Sanjay. "You have better medicine than we do."

"Because we have tested them, and they don't. As you said, we have better medicine than you do." Sanjay was giving him no quarter. "These boys are members of your village and your family. They deserve your attention and your care. These doctors are willing to give them their care if you will not help them."

The woman who'd opened the door stepped out into the courtyard. She walked over to Alex with footsteps that barely made a sound and stood next to him. Alex looked at the woman, and the flash of fire that blazed in her eyes for just a few seconds was almost enough to have Dillon take a step back. He figured she was Alex's wife, but damn....

"All right. I will speak to the men."

"I will speak to the women," she said. "We'll talk reason. Tomorrow we will bring the boys home." She glared at Alex, and he turned back to them and nodded. It seemed the question had been settled.

"Thank you," Dillon said. "The youngest, Wamah, hasn't been talking at all. He's grieving a lot."

She nodded and stood a little taller. Damn, she was statuesque. "We will care for them like we should have all along." And damn if she didn't seem to be daring Alex to contradict her.

"Thank you both," Dillon said gently and then turned to leave. He'd gotten what he came for and was ready to leave before he said something that blew the whole thing. He was still angry that they'd had to do this in the first place. But the thought of that one little word—"we"—was enough to make him forget all about that and want to shout from the rooftop. Of course it could have been just Will's way of making his point.

Sanjay and Will stayed a few minutes and then followed Dillon out to the car. "Juna will come over tomorrow to get the boys, and Alex and his wife have assured us that they will speak to the appropriate people," Sanjay said.

"Do you really think they can change people's minds?" Dillon asked as he pulled open the door and got in the stiflingly hot backseat.

"If Alex's wife has anything to say about it, then, yeah, I think it will," Sanjay said as he got in his seat and closed the door. He started the engine while Will got in as well, and they rode back to the hospital. "I'll leave it to the two of you to explain what's going on to the boys. This should be very good news for them." He turned to Will. "That was quite a bluff you ran, and one hell of a chance you took with that whole adoption story. I know it brought the point home that you weren't afraid, but what if he'd called you on it?"

"It wasn't a bluff," Dillon said. "I did talk about it." He lightly touched Will's shoulder. "It didn't go any further than talk, and Will and I figured that the boys would be better in a place they were familiar with. Wamah isn't talking, and I can only imagine that a move to the other side of the world, where nothing is the same, wouldn't be good for him."

Sanjay turned to glance at Will and then looked ahead once again. Dillon wasn't sure how much Sanjay had figured out, not that it really mattered at this point. "So you were prepared for an instant family?"

"I wasn't, but I would have done it anyway."

Will turned and smiled at him quickly. The knot that had twisted in Dillon's belly for the past day or so finally began to unravel. "Yeah."

Sanjay just shook his head. Dillon wasn't going to press anything at this moment. He was too damned happy. When they arrived at the hospital compound, he and Will went to find the boys. Topka and Kparsi were playing ball while Wamah once again sat in the shade of a tree, looking just as miserable as before.

"So," Topka demanded, catching the ball and then walking over.

"Juna will be here tomorrow to take you back home with her," Dillon explained. "The village leader and his wife are both in your corner, and they've agreed to help."

"Juna will not get threats because of us?" Topka said.

"I can't guarantee that, because people are afraid. But they have agreed to help you," Will said.

"You did this for us?" Topka asked.

"Of course," Dillon said. "We want you to be happy and to have a home. Why wouldn't we? All three of you are important to us. You're my friend."

Topka smiled and then turned and gave the others the news. Wamah stood and joined them. He didn't talk, but he appeared less dejected, even if he stayed close to his brother. Dillon had the idea that Wamah needed more than time to get over what had happened, but he wouldn't get it. He reminded himself to talk to Sanjay. Though even if a counselor were to come in, it wasn't as though the locals would speak with them. At least the two older boys, hurt as they were, were paying attention to him.

"Are you going to stay out here?" Dillon asked.

"Yes," Kparsi answered. "We'll stay in the compound."

"And come in for dinner," Dillon told them. "Dr. Will and I will look for you." He turned, and they walked toward the hospital.

"Thank you," Wamah called from behind them.

Dillon swallowed hard and turned around. "You're welcome," he said with a smile and then continued on in to go to work.

BY THE time Dillon had had dinner and finished with his patients, including helping to stitch a wound on a youngster who'd fallen and cut his arm open on a rock, he was too tired to keep his eyes open. But the day had been a success in almost every way. He was still cautious about the boys and would feel better once Juna arrived. Otherwise, he was pleased. He checked that the boys were settled in for the night and then went to the room. Will was waiting for him with a worried expression.

"What is it?"

"Nothing. I think I'm worried about crap."

"Why?" Dillon closed the door and sat on the edge of his bed. "What are you nervous about?" Suddenly Dillon was concerned.

"What I said earlier about adopting the boys. That could have backfired so badly."

"You didn't mean it?" Dillon asked. Much of the exuberance and joy that had carried him through the day went up in smoke.

"Of course I meant it."

"You know you said 'we,'" Dillon said hopefully, praying it hadn't been a mistake or something said in the heat of the moment.

"Yes, I did, and I meant it. If Alex had refused to help those kids, I don't know what would have happened, but I wasn't going to walk away. I was wrong yesterday, and you aren't the only one whose heart was touched by them. I just didn't want to admit it."

"You really meant that there is a 'we'?" Dillon knew he was being daft, but he needed clarity.

"Yes. There's a 'we' for as long as you want one."

That was all Dillon needed to hear. "So we should make plans for when we go home. My friends will be thrilled to meet you, and I can call the hospital and talk to the administration."

"What about opening the practice you talked about?"

Dillon paused. "Is that what you really want?

"I think so. I've had more than enough working in hospitals, at least for the time being. I think I want to work with individuals in a more quiet setting."

"Then, children… you know they aren't quiet."

"You know what I mean," Will said, laughing softly.

"I do." He stood and went to sit next to Will. "This is really going to happen." God, he hoped he didn't get all bouncy the way he used to when he was a kid.

"Yes. It's really going to happen." Will's smile was luminous. He turned to Dillon and moved closer. Within seconds, he was pressing Dillon back on the bed. "I think we have to celebrate." Will turned away and yawned. "Man…."

"It's okay. How about we celebrate when both of us can keep our eyes open? Besides, there will be more to celebrate once the boys are truly home and neither of us is bone-tired."

Will nodded, and Dillon pulled him down into a kiss that, while tender, held little heat, simply because neither of them could muster it. Then they got ready for bed and turned out the lights, finding each other's hands in the dark.

"I never expected to meet someone," Dillon whispered.

"I'd long ago given up on it. I figured there wasn't anyone out there for me."

"I guess we were both wrong."

Will chuckled in the darkness. "I think that's one of the first times I'm glad to have been mistaken." Will tightened his hold on Dillon's hand and grew quiet.

Chapter 11

THE WEEKS seemed to run by in a flurry of activity. Juna did pick up the boys, and they stopped by the hospital once a week to say hello and play soccer. They seemed happier every week, though Dillon figured there would be a long climb back to the joy and excitement he'd seen during those very first games. Dillon hoped they would get there, but knew it would take a lot of time.

"Tomorrow is my last official day off before we leave. Do you think we could go back to the ocean?" Dillon asked Will one night once they were in bed. Somehow he actually found the energy to speak after Will had spent the last hour wearing him out.

"I think we can do that." Will paused. "Do you want to see if the boys want to go too? I know it won't be romantic, but I'm sure they could use a day of fun."

Dillon sat up and leaned over Will. "You're an amazing man." He kissed him. "I think that would be amazing."

"Okay. Then we'll make plans in the morning." Will squeezed his hand, and the next thing Dillon knew, the sun was shining through the window.

Dillon dressed and hurried through his morning routine, checking on things at the hospital before meeting Will and the boys out by the gate. All three of them were excited—even Wamah was smiling. Will got them all into one of the old hospital vans, and they took off down the same roads he and Dillon had traveled before. They seemed even worse this time, and Dillon was more than ready to get there.

They parked at the beach and opened the doors. Shoes came off, and the boys let out a loud whoop as they raced toward the water. Dillon came around the van and stood next to Will, watching as all three of them hit the water with yells and cries of happiness. "This was so worth it," Dillon whispered, and Will nodded his agreement. "Didn't Juna want to come?"

"I think she wanted a day of quiet," Will said, turning to him with a small smile.

"I don't blame her," Dillon admitted as Kparsi crashed into Topka, taking him under the water. Both boys came up with more laughter. They never seemed to stop. Wamah stayed in the shallows, but he seemed to be having fun and eventually settled down to dig in the sand. "They're like Energizer Bunnies."

"Yes, they are. It's great to see." Will opened the back and pulled out the umbrella and blanket, then handed them to Dillon. He got the food they'd brought for lunch and then closed the door. Together, the two of them walked across the sand to a good place. There were other people on the beach today, so they kept their distance. Not that they wouldn't have with the boys around. He and Will had always been careful around them, unsure if they'd understand.

Dillon spread the blanket and set up the umbrella. Then he pulled off his shoes and raced into the surf. The boys joined him, and Dillon was completely wet before he even reached his waist, all three boys sending up a wall of spray. Will joined them, and it was a miracle there was any water left in the ocean by the time they all got done splashing and carrying on. Dillon couldn't stay in too long because of the strong sun, so he was the first to get out and sit on the blanket in the shade. Will continued to play and have fun. Dillon expected Will would join him soon, but it was Topka who eventually came to sit next to him on the blanket.

"You are leaving," he said.

"Yes. It's almost time for Dr. Will and me to go home." Dillon swallowed and didn't dare look at him for fear the sadness that threatened to overwhelm him would show on his face.

"Will you be doctors there?" Topka asked. Dillon thought it a strange question. "I mean, in a place like here?"

"I don't know. We've talked about opening an office to help kids."

"Like us?" Topka asked.

"Yes, in a way. There are sick children in America too, and I think I'd like to be able to try to help them get better."

"Do you help them like you helped us?" Dillon wasn't sure what Topka was asking. "Will you play soccer with them?"

"No. You three are the only ones I play soccer with," Dillon said and finally got up the courage to look at Topka. "You're all good boys, and I want you to be happy." God, that sounded dumb to him as soon as he said it, but it was what he was feeling, so to hell with it.

"Will you miss us?" Topka asked as Kparsi ran out of the water toward them. Will scooped Wamah up and carried the laughing youngster over.

"Yes. I'll miss all of you very much." Damn, he hadn't thought about how hard this was going to be. Thankfully, Will sat Wamah down and helped him dry off, and after using his towel, Kparsi dropped onto the blanket, and they proceeded to eat a raucous lunch that made Dillon forget what he was going to be losing for a little while. Soon he would say good-bye to three young friends who had worked their way into his heart. It wasn't likely he'd ever see them again, but Dillon knew he'd never forget them. The three boys had given him something he never expected to find: a sense that life was short and that no matter what, he needed to find the joy in it. And the primary source of his newfound joy sat just across from him on the blanket with drops of water running down his sleek chest, a warm smile on his face, a smile meant just for him. Of course, he was the only one who knew that particular piece of information.

"Eat so you don't get worn out in the water," Will chided him, and Dillon looked at his plate, realizing he'd let his mind wander and hadn't been paying attention. He'd come to Liberia to advance his career and gain some unique experience, but what he'd actually gotten was so much more.

The boys laughed, and Dillon realized his food was going to slip off his plate.

"He's messy like you," Kparsi teased his brother, and Dillon straightened his plate and went back to eating. There would be plenty of time for woolgathering over the next week. Right now they were at the beach, and it was time for fun.

Wamah pushed Kparsi back, and the brothers had an argument in a language Dillon didn't understand, but the brotherly teasing back and forth translated well enough.

"I'm going to finish eating, and then we'll hit the water once again." Dillon finished his lunch and then helped put everything away. Without thinking, he then grabbed Will's hand and they raced into the water with the boys right behind, all of them yelling, their happiness mixing with the sound of the waves and carried away on the wind. It was glorious and something he'd hold in his heart forever.

THE REST of the remaining week went by so fast that Dillon barely had a chance to think. Before he knew it, his things were packed and loaded into the back of the van, sitting next to Will's. He'd said good-bye to everyone he'd worked with, and there had been sniffles and a few choked-back tears. "I was hoping to be able to say good-bye to the boys," Dillon said as he closed the van door and looked for the millionth time toward the gate to the hospital compound.

"I know," Will told him.

Dillon hadn't seen the boys since their trip to the beach. Juna had insisted that all three of them go to school and had apparently, with the help of Alex's wife, shamed the local leader into paying for it.

"The boys are in school, where they should be." Will climbed in the van with Dillon behind him. "Their lives are moving on, and so is yours."

Just as Dillon was about to close the door, Wamah raced through the gate with the others, including Juna, close behind him. Dillon got out and met them, hugging them all at once. Up till now he'd kept his distance physically, but he wasn't holding back now. "I'm going to miss all of you," Dillon said and hugged each of the boys in turn.

"Thank you for everything," Topka said when Dillon hugged him.

"You take care of them," Dillon told him.

"I will," Topka said and then hugged Dillon back.

"We need to go or we'll miss our flight," Will said, and the boys descended on him, each taking a turn.

"Thank you both," Juna whispered with a smile once everyone stood back. "I'll care for them like my own family."

"I know you will," Dillon told her. "Thank you." He wasn't sure what else to say, so he turned and got back in the van. He waited for Will and gave a final wave as the driver pulled out and went through the gate. He and Will began the journey home and the start of their new life together.

THE PLANE trip home was grueling, as was the reception they received in Chicago. They were grilled and their health was checked. There had been talk of a mandatory three-week quarantine, but that didn't seem to be a requirement. Neither of them had been in contact with Ebola patients for the past two weeks. Sanjay had insisted on it, and since a number of new doctors had arrived, they'd spent their time with other patients.

"We missed our connection," Will said, staring up at the flight schedule board once they'd been allowed to leave the isolation area.

"It's all right. I made a call while you were being cleared, and there's a car waiting for us," Dillon said. "We need to go to baggage claim to get our luggage. It should be there by now, and then we can go home." God, those words sounded wonderful. "This way."

By the time they made it to the airline baggage-claim office, their luggage was waiting for them, and they headed outside into the crisp early autumn air. The slight chill was more than welcome, and Dillon took a deep breath and released it. "I believe this is ours," Dillon said as a limousine pulled up to the curb. The driver took their luggage and placed it in the trunk while he and Will got in back.

"This isn't really necessary," Will said with a smile as he looked over the interior.

"Sure it is," Dillon said and scooted right next to Will, pulling him close. "It's essential," Dillon said as his gaze locked on Will's.

"Are we still talking about the car?" Will whispered.

"What do you think?" Dillon leaned closer, capturing Will's lips as the car pulled away from the curb. "I can't wait to be able to sleep in the same bed with you and have you wake up next to me."

Will chuckled. "I'm not going to miss the twin beds, and all I can say is thank God for air-conditioning, and you. Most definitely you."

They stayed close the entire ride. After spending all that time together but having to be careful about every touch, Dillon took advantage of the privacy and held Will close the entire time. He never wanted to let him go and didn't intend to for a long time. The ride took a couple hours, and by the time they pulled up in front of Dillon's house, they were both half asleep. It didn't matter that it was two in the afternoon; they had been traveling for more than a day.

Dillon fished out his keys, and the driver helped carry the luggage inside. As soon as Dillon had tipped him and he was on his way, with the door closed and locked, Dillon took Will's arm and led him up the stairs. "The bathroom is here, and the kitchen and living room are downstairs."

"Aren't you going to show me around, since I'm going to live here?"

Dillon grabbed the base of Will's shirt, then pulled it up and off. "The bedroom is right over there." He tugged Will into a kiss and heard him mumble something about seeing his point, and that was all. They fumbled their way into the bedroom and down onto his king-size bed, both of them sighing as the mattress cradled them. "God, I missed this," Dillon sighed.

"The bed or me?" Will asked with a wry grin that Dillon proceeded to kiss away.

"You. Always you," Dillon whispered and gasped softly when Will slid his hand under his shirt. "I love you so damn much." He kissed him again. Will rolled Dillon onto his back and made slow love to him until they were both so wrung out that they fell asleep, not noticing when the sun faded and the windows darkened. Dillon woke at some point in the night and pulled Will close, and they made love again, getting to know each other in the darkness.

THEY WOKE to a ringing phone. Dillon jumped and tried to figure out what the hell the sound was. He reached to the bedside table and managed to pick it up without knocking everything off. "Hello."

"Dillon, it's your mother. I see you made it home," she said.

"Yes. We got home yesterday and went right to bed." Dillon rolled over, and Will shifted in the bed next to him. "I was going to call you today."

"Who is we?" his mother asked.

"I told you about Will, remember? He's here with me."

"Yes, the other doctor who was coming back with you. Since you're awake, and I'm free for lunch, I was hoping I could see you."

Dillon sighed and wondered how he could get out of it. There was no way, and he resigned himself to his fate. "All right. Where do you want to meet?" He rolled over to look at the clock.

"The club, of course, at noon," his mother said as though he should be able to read her mind.

"Fine. Will and I will meet you there." Dillon hung up before she could say anything else.

"Where are we going?" Will asked sleepily.

"My mother wants to meet for lunch."

Will sat up and wiped the sleep from his eyes. "You want me to go with you? Why don't you go, and I'll... I don't know, keep myself busy somehow."

"No. I want you to come along."

"To meet your mother."

"I want you to be part of my life, so, yeah, that means meeting my mother. I know it'll be a trial by fire, but I really want you to come with me." Dillon sat up as well. "You don't have to, but I'd like it if you did."

Will nodded slowly. "What if she doesn't like me?"

"I refuse to say something as cliché as that my mother is going to love you, because I have no idea how she's going to react. That's the fun part. But she's too well-mannered to ever be anything other than polite and nice in public."

"Fine," Will said, getting out of bed. Dillon watched as Will's butt bounced slightly on his way to the bathroom. "I'll come along. I've heard so much about your mother, I have to see for myself." Will disappeared into the bathroom, and Dillon looked at the clock once again and got up as well. He put on his robe and went downstairs to haul up the luggage. He went in the bedroom and put Will's soiled clothes in the hamper.

Once Will came out of the bathroom, he took his turn and poked his head out of the door. "I'm going to shower. Do you want to join me?"

Dillon had rarely seen Will move so quickly. Dillon started the water, and once it warmed, they stepped together under the spray. "God, I love how you feel, especially wet." Dillon pressed his chest to Will's back and ran his hands up and down his belly. "We didn't get to do things like this before," Dillon whispered.

"I know. It feels nice." Will leaned his head back against Dillon's shoulder, and Dillon let his hands wander until they cupped Will's balls and circled around his cock. Dillon stroked slowly, taking time to savor the wonder of having Will in his home—well, their home now.

"It does. But we do need to get moving if we don't want to be late." Dillon continued stroking, ignoring his own warning.

"God, the last thing I want is to be late when I meet your mother."

Dillon let his hands fall away. Nothing killed the mood quite like the mention of his mother. Granted, it was his own fault and he knew he should have kept his mouth shut. They washed each other and stood under the water until it began to cool. Dillon turned off the shower and stepped out, grabbing the towels he'd set out. He handed Will his and quickly explained where everything was in the bathroom. "You can have this shelf in the medicine cabinet, and there's a shelf in the linen closet that's empty as well. I need to bring in a dresser for your clothes, but there's closet space for you too."

"I take it you don't have a bunch of extra clothes," Will said when they got back into the bedroom and began dressing. Dillon opened the closet to show him.

"I don't feel the need for a lot of extra things. So take the space you need."

Will chuckled. "Everything I own is in those two suitcases. I think I'll have more than enough room." Will bent down to lift one of the suitcases and his towel fell to the floor.

Dillon whistled softly. "I can't believe you're here." It was almost unfathomable that a wonderful guy like Will had fallen in love with him.

Will simply shook his head and began getting dressed.

Dillon did the same, and when they both had their shoes on, Dillon led Will downstairs and gave him a brief tour of the house, showing him where things were. "When I decorated the house, I wanted it to be comfortable. I didn't go for anything really fancy."

"I like it. Everything is simple and masculine." Will sat in one of the leather chairs in the living room and put his feet up on the ottoman. "God, I could sit here all day."

"I'm glad you're comfortable, because I want this to feel like your home. I know it will seem strange because everything in here is mine, but we need another chair for the living room, so we can pick out one you like." Dillon leaned over the back of the chair, and Will looked up. Dillon kissed him, heat building fast. "If I keep doing that, we'll definitely be late."

Will put his feet down and stood up. Dillon got his keys and led Will out the back door toward the garage. He opened the door and let Will go ahead.

He whistled. "Wow. Are these your cars?" Will walked around the BMW, then ran his hand lightly over the hood of Dillon's original Mustang convertible.

"Yeah," Dillon said. "When we get back, you can take her out for a spin if you like."

Will lifted his gaze. "You'd let me drive it?" That "kid in a candy store" tone was precious.

"Sure," Dillon responded. "But for now we need to get going." He unlocked the doors of the BMW and got inside, pressing the button on the garage door opener. Once Will was buckled in the passenger seat, Dillon backed out of the garage, closed the door, and then headed toward the freeway.

"What's your mother really like? Should we stop somewhere so I can get flowers?" Will shifted nervously in his seat. "I guess I expected I'd have more time before I met your parents."

"We've known each other and been close for almost three months. We saw each other every day, worked together, and lived together. I don't think this is particularly quick, given what you and I have already done."

"What have we done? I mean, we were working."

"We did more than that. We helped Kparsi, Topka, and Wamah find a home and helped see them through their loss. You saw me through that scare and never left my side." Dillon pulled onto the freeway and picked up speed. "I'll never forget you in the ocean that first time, the way you looked at me. It was like I was the only one who mattered in the entire world. No one's looked at me like that before... and I see that in you every day." Will placed his hand on Dillon's thigh and squeezed lightly. "See? Just like that."

"Yeah, but...."

"There's nothing to be worried about. I look at you the same way." Dillon smiled and continued the drive up to River Hills. He got off the freeway and continued on the secondary roads to the gates of the club. He pulled in and up to the clubhouse while Will watched out the window.

"Jesus," Will mumbled. "This is like nothing I've ever seen before."

Dillon saw Will glance down at his clothes and then run his hands nervously over his pant legs. "Do I look right for this?"

"You look fine. Besides, wait until you see the older men in their golf pants. You'll wish you had sunglasses, even indoors. The bright colors are supposed to help you be seen on the course, at least that's how they started, but I really think that half the men are color blind and have no idea how ridiculous they look."

Will smiled, and Dillon opened his door. He handed his keys to the valet and then joined Will before escorting him inside and toward the restaurant.

"Dr. McDowell," the host said with a smile. "Your mother is expecting you...." He looked at Will in surprise. "She asked for a table for two."

"I'd appreciate it if you could move us to a larger table." Dillon kept the annoyance out of his voice. He had told her he was bringing Will.

"Of course. Right this way."

They followed him, and as they approached the small table where his mother sat, she stood and at least had the grace to look surprised when she saw Will. "Honey, I didn't know you were bringing a friend."

Dillon ground his teeth and leaned closer to offer the cheek kiss she expected. "You knew perfectly well I was bringing someone, and you'd better be nice." She gasped slightly, and Dillon met her gaze and held it until she looked away. "We're being moved to another table." He turned to Will. "Mom, I'd like you to meet Dr. William Scarlet. He and I worked together in Liberia, and he's going to stay with me... permanently. Will, this is my mother, Suzanne McDowell."

They shook hands, and the host arranged for them to be reseated. Will seemed uncomfortable and kept looking around. Dillon's mother glanced at everything except them, and Dillon's temper began to rise.

"Where are your manners?" he hissed to her while Will read his menu.

She had the grace to look shocked. She sipped her wine and then set down the glass. "So what sort of doctor are you?" she asked Will. "Do you have a specialty?"

"Family medicine," Will answered. "I've been working overseas for much of my career. I was in Liberia with Dillon, and Kenya for a while before that. Most of the time I've been in Africa."

"Where's your home?"

"With Dillon," Will answered without missing a beat, and Dillon squeezed Will's hand under the table.

"Will's family doesn't accept him, so he's been on his own for a while."

That seemed to get through his mother's façade. "You don't see them? Ever?"

"My mom made their wishes perfectly clear a number of years ago. I wrote to them for a while, but never heard anything." Will picked up his water glass and gulped. Dillon turned to his mother, raising his eyebrow, daring her to say something mean. Instead, she surprised him.

"That's terrible." She set down her glass. "Goodness knows, Dillon's father and I aren't perfect parents, but we'd never disown him or turn our backs on him. He's our son." She raised her gaze and caught the server's eye. "Yes, I think the young man here could use something stronger than water, and I'd like some more wine. Dillon?"

"Just a soda. I'm driving," Dillon told the server. "Will, order whatever you'd like."

Will ordered a glass of wine, and the conversation resumed once the server left.

"What are your plans now that you're back?"

"Dillon and I talked about opening a practice. We both want to work with children. But we'll see how things go. For now I'm going to apply at the hospital. I have a lot of experience with exotic diseases. At least they're exotic here."

"Was it hard working there?" his mother asked.

The server approached to take their orders.

Dillon waited until they'd placed their orders and the server had left again. "Yes, it was, Mom."

"That must take dedication."

"Mom, Will is an Ebola survivor. He got the disease helping other people and survived it. So, yeah, it does take dedication." He locked gazes with Will. "And a hell of a lot more than that. It takes an internal strength I never knew I had, but Will was there to make sure I got it." Dillon swallowed. "We were a good team, and I don't think I could have done it without him."

She said nothing. There were times when his mother's expression was like an open book and those, like now, when she was impossible to gauge.

"I wrote you that I got sick."

"Yes, and it wasn't Ebola," his mother said quickly.

"It wasn't. Will worked hard to confirm that and took care of me in the meantime."

"We weren't sure for a while, and we had to take precautions," Will interjected rather tentatively.

"Mom," Dillon began again. "He rarely left my side until we knew exactly what was going on and I was well on my way to recovery." Dillon figured he might as well continue on. "He loves me and I love him."

"But you've only known each other for a few months. How can you be sure that—" Her voice remained remarkably steady.

"Mom, I've been very sure for quite some time. It's you who won't accept the truth. And I won't have you interfering with our lives or excluding Will the way you tried to do today—and don't deny it. He's an important part of my life." Dillon kept his voice as soft and gentle as possible.

"I don't understand any of this," his mother said and picked up her purse. She opened it and pulled out a tissue from the Gucci bag that cost more than the annual income of the entire village in Liberia. "All I want is for you to be like everyone else. Is that so bad?"

Dillon didn't know what to say.

"He is like everyone else," Will said, and Dillon's mother paused with her tissue near her eyes. "It took me a while to figure things out so I could put words to them, but Dillon and I aren't any different from anyone else. We both want and deserve love, we care for each other, we want to make a living, and have a home. We want a family… heck, we talked about adopting children when we were in Liberia. Mrs. McDowell, Dillon and I have talked about just about everything. Just because one of us isn't a woman doesn't mean we're different from anyone else. And wishing Dillon were something he isn't is hurtful."

His mother remained still for a moment and then turned to him. "I never thought of it that way."

"I know, Mom. Sometimes we all get single-minded in what we want or think is best, and we forget what's important." Dillon knew he was letting her off the hook, but he was fine with that.

"Would you excuse me a minute?" Will said and stood up, then back the way they'd come in toward the restrooms.

"So this is for real? The two of you?" his mother asked, following Will with her gaze. "He seems like a nice enough young man."

"Yes, it's for real, and yes, he's way more than nice." Dillon took a drink of his soda. "I want you and Dad to like him. It's important to me, but I think it's even more important to him. Think of it as standing in for parents everywhere. His own have turned their backs on him, and let's face it, you were never going to be nominated for mother of the year." Dillon hardened his gaze. "But this is your chance to make a clean start with him and with me." It was time he let go of the baggage he'd been carrying for years. It wasn't doing him any good, and in the grand scheme of things, it didn't matter. The past was the past; what mattered was now and the time they had together.

"What changed with you?" his mother asked rather haltingly, like she was wondering if Dillon was for real.

"I've seen children die of diseases that kids here would shrug off easily. Parents who die within days of each other, orphaning entire families. Poverty that would ensure you never needed another perm for the rest of your life. And those people find ways to laugh and make the most of the time they're given." Dillon thought for a second and began speaking faster, needing to say what he wanted before Will returned. "They have nothing and yet they make the most of each day they have. Family is so important to them, and so is compassion and community. I want that in my life, and I need it for Will."

"Jesus…," his mother whispered half under her breath, and then she did the last thing Dillon expected—she smiled. "Yes, I think it's time we all made an effort." She paused pensively. "I'm proud of you."

"You are?" Dillon was shocked; there was no other way to express it. His mother ordered, cajoled, even crocodile-teared, and of course, guilt was the ultimate Howitzer in her arsenal, but sincerity was completely new.

"I've always been proud of your accomplishments, but it's time I told you I'm proud of the man you've become." A hug was too much to expect, but she did pat his hand lightly before picking up her glass of wine. Will returned to the table and sat down once again. "So, Dr. Scarlet, I'm having a benefit next week for the children's hospital, and you and Dillon must come. Everyone will be so interested in hearing about your experiences, and nothing gets them to open their wallets faster than real stories of need and hope." She smiled.

Dillon swallowed hard. It was a first step, but a big one. The server brought small salads, and while Will was eating his, Dillon leaned toward his mother. "I'm proud of you too." They shared a brief look, and damn if he didn't see a tear or two. Then he sat straight once again and went back to his lunch.

They talked steadily through the remainder of the meal, with Will opening up a little more as the minutes passed and the wine flowed. When they got up to leave, she invited both of them back to the house.

"Don't you have a meeting?" Dillon asked. She always seemed to either be in a hurry to get to one or was hosting one at the house.

"No. I'd like to get to know Will better." She threaded her arm through his, and Dillon shook his head and thanked his lucky stars. Dillon didn't think Will was ready for the full-on McDowell mansion right now. The slightly glazed look in his eyes said that he was starting to get a little overwhelmed.

"We can come to lunch again, but I think now we're both still very tired from all the travel. I promise we'll see you soon." Dillon leaned down and kissed his mother's cheek, and she let go of Will's arm once the valet brought her car around.

"I'm going to hold you to that," she said with a smile and got in her car, waving slightly before pulling away.

"That was not what I expected," Will commented as Dillon handed his slip to the valet.

"Me either," Dillon said with a smile. "You charmed her, big-time, and I really think she likes you. I also figured you'd probably had enough of my mother for the afternoon." The car pulled under the portico, and Dillon walked to the driver's side and tipped the valet before getting in.

"She's a huge personality."

"That she is." Dillon leaned across the seat, not caring in the least who saw, and kissed Will on the lips, sliding his hand around the back of his neck to deepen the kiss slightly. "I also want some time with you."

"Alone time?" Will asked with a smile.

"I was thinking *bed* time to be more specific."

"Perfect. How fast can we get home?"

Instead of answering, Dillon pulled out and went as fast as he dared the entire trip back to the house. After pulling into the garage, they hurried into the house, and as soon as the door closed behind them, Will had him pressed against the refrigerator door. Fuck, he felt good pressed against him. Their tongues and lips dueled for supremacy for a few seconds until Dillon made a strategic surrender and was rewarded when Will pulled him back, grabbing his ass through his pants. Dillon moaned loudly, and Will kissed it away, ramping up the heat.

"Let's go upstairs," Will whispered against his lips. "Either that or I'm going to take you right here on the floor."

"Damn. What did I do to earn this?"

"Just being you," Will whispered as he manhandled him toward the kitchen door.

Since Dillon wasn't particularly interested in the hard floor, he scrambled up the stairs with Will right behind him. By the time he reached the bedroom, his shirt had been left behind and his pants were pooled around his ankles. He stumbled onto the bed with Will scrambling to catch up.

"Has anyone ever told you how sexy you are?" Will asked.

Dillon held Will's cheeks in his hands. "Maybe a few times, but I could hear it again and again."

"How about for the rest of our lives?" Will asked.

"Okay, but you know a life with me comes with my parents and plenty of lunches like today."

"Are you trying to warn me off or is this a bargaining session? Because if we're bargaining, then my demands are plenty of time alone in bed, at least two kids, a home together, and a dog. I want it all—a life and home filled with love, and you."

Dillon wanted those things too, and he tugged Will closer. "Sold." Then he kissed him hard.

Epilogue

"DILLON!" WILL called as he came through the back door. "There are flowers in the yard." Excitement filled the house. "I was beginning to think I was never going to be warm again." Dillon heard Will's footsteps in the kitchen above him. He made sure his surprise was all set and then hurried upstairs from the basement. "Where are you?"

"Just taking care of a few things," Dillon answered as he came up the stairs. "How was your day?"

"Busy," Will told him with a grin. "Milton asked me today if I'd given any thought to going back to Liberia. Apparently Doctors Without Borders contacted him again."

"What did you tell him?" Dillon asked. They had talked things over the first time Will had been asked, but not since. "You know if you want to go, I'll be here waiting for you when you get back."

Will stepped closer, his smile brightening, eyes dancing in the sunlight streaming through the kitchen windows. "I know, and it's tempting, but I told them no, thank you. I did my part—we've done our part. Now it's someone else's turn."

Dillon was ashamed at how happy that answer made him. He would definitely have supported Will's decision, but he hated the thought of Will being gone for months. They had asked Dillon as well, but it just wasn't possible at this point. His patient load had skyrocketed in the past six months, and with the opening of his own practice just a few months away, there was just too much for him to do. People were counting on him, and he wasn't going to let them down. The plan was still for Will to join him, but Dillon was willing to cover for him if he wanted to go.

"You seem relieved," Will observed. He rarely seemed to miss much when it came to Dillon.

"Call me selfish, but I don't want you to go. I like coming home knowing you'll be here and having you to spend time with." The truth was he knew he'd worry every second Will was gone.

"Then I'm the same, because I don't want to spend months without you either." Will pulled him into a hug. "Do we have time before this thing at your mother's?" He waggled his eyebrows slightly. The social invitations had begun to run together a little. "What is it for?"

"Tonight is the local humane society," Dillon answered. "And I'm afraid we need to get changed and ready to go. At least it's casual tonight."

"All right, I'll head up to change." Will kissed him and then bounded up the stairs. Dillon watched him go and then hurried back into the basement. The golden/lab mix puppy stared up at him, his little tail wagging like crazy. Dillon lifted him into his arms and carried him up both sets of stairs. He saw Will in their bedroom in only his boxers. Dillon whistled when Will stripped them off and turned around. "What's this?"

"Mom asked me to stop by the shelter on my way home to pick up some fliers, and this little guy caught my eye." He moved closer and held the puppy so Will could pet him. "I got him for you." He handed the wriggling puppy to Will, who was instantly covered in wet puppy kisses. "I know we said we wanted to wait a little while for kids, but I thought I'd start the family with this little guy."

"He isn't going to be little for long," Will said with a smile that turned to laughter as the puppy's tail thumped Will's chest. Does he have a name?"

"Nope. That's your job." Dillon reached for the energetic ball of fur.

"What are we going to do with him while we're gone?" Will asked. "Maybe I should stay home."

"It's the humane society benefit—he's invited. My mother is apparently looking forward to meeting her grandpuppy, and if I show up without her favorite son-in-law, I think I'll be lynched, so go get your shower while I take him outside to do his puppy business, and then I'll get dressed."

Dillon headed down the stairs and out the back door, thankful the backyard was already fenced. He set the puppy down, and he ran off to explore. Dillon watched him poke around the shrubs and then bound toward the large tree that shaded the yard when one of the squirrels made an appearance. A few yips and the squirrel was gone, the puppy attempting to climb the tree after it. Dillon laughed and waited for him to finish his business before coaxing the puppy inside.

Will met them at the base of the stairs and took the puppy to play while Dillon cleaned up and changed.

Half an hour later, Will, Dillon, and Topka Jr. were in the Mustang. Will drove, and Dillon held the puppy in his arms so he could look out the window. They pulled into the drive, and the valets his mother had hired took the keys as they got out. They were early but expected. The yard was decked out with tents, tables, candles, lanterns, heaters for warmth, and enough flowers to open three flower shops. The Italianate fountain out near the road had been uncovered and awakened from its winter slumber.

"Sweetheart," his mother called as she came out the front door to greet them. Both he and Will were greeted warmly. Things had come a long way among the three of them. His father was still his father, and he remained aloof and obsessed with business, but there were no further attempts at matchmaking, and Dillon was hopeful that spring might bring a thaw other than the weather. "You did bring him."

"Of course. You said he was invited," Dillon reminded her, and the puppy smacked his mother across the face with a big old lick.

"That's enough," she said lightly. "You don't want a tongue full of makeup."

Other cars pulled into the drive, and his mother went into full hostess mode. She took the puppy from Dillon and went to greet the first of her guests.

"Did she just commandeer our puppy?" Will asked.

"Of course," his mother's voice drifted out over the lawn. "This is Dillon's and Will's new puppy. They just adopted him from the shelter. Isn't he adorable?"

"Yes, but all for a good cause. She's a pro at extracting money for her causes." Dillon began to chuckle uncontrollably. "That will last until she finds out that puppies make puddles." He took Will's hand. "Come on, we need to mingle with the guests, and I'll rescue my mother's dress." They walked over to where his mother was talking, and Dillon slipped Topka Jr. out of her arms. He got out the leash he'd brought and put it on the puppy's collar before putting him down and letting him prance around in the grass.

"Yes. That's my grandpuppy," Dillon's mother said as she greeted some more new arrivals. "For now it's as close to grandchildren as I'm going to get."

"She isn't subtle, is she?" Will asked.

"Nope," Dillon said and moved closer to Will. "But she can wait a little while longer. I want you all to myself for a while."

Will pulled his phone out of his pocket and stared at the screen, breaking into a smile. "I think it's my turn to give you a present." Will turned the phone so he could see it. Three boys grinned at him, the youngest holding a soccer ball. "Sanjay said to tell you that Topka, Kparsi, and Wamah are doing well and seem to be thriving. They're all in school, and Wamah apparently wants to be a doctor just like Dr. Dillon."

Dillon swallowed hard and turned away.

"Do you remember in medical school when we were naïve and thought we could change the world? Well, you let your spirit free and you changed their world and mine." Will pulled him closer and kissed him. "It doesn't get better than that."

Dillon couldn't agree more, and judging by his happy yip, the puppy agreed too.

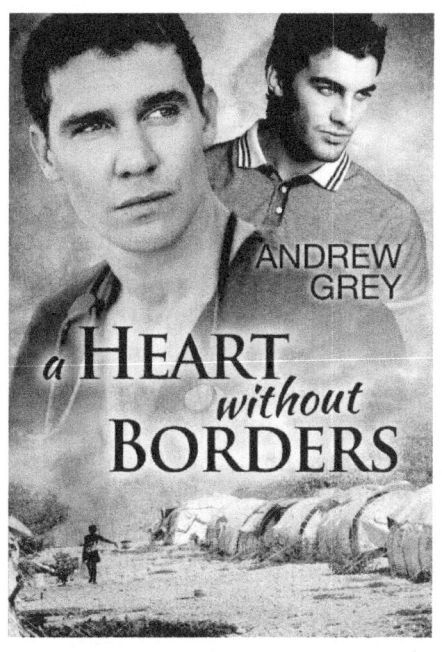

Pediatrician Wes Gordon will do just about anything to escape his grief. When opportunity knocks, he signs on to work at a hospital in a tent camp in Haiti. One night while returning to his quarters, he comes across a gang of kids attempting to set fire to an underage rentboy and intervenes, taking the injured René under his wing. At the hospital, diplomat Anthony Crowley tells Wes that the kids involved in the attack are from prominent families and trying to hold them responsible will cause a firestorm.

In spite of the official position Anthony must take, Wes's compassion captures his attention. Anthony pursues him, and they grow closer during the stolen moments between Anthony's assignments, escaping earthquake destruction for glimpses of Caribbean paradise. When Wes realizes the only way to save René is to adopt him, Anthony is supportive, but time is running out: Wes must leave the country, and Anthony is called out on a dangerous secret mission. Now Wes must face adopting a boy from Haiti who has no papers without the support of the one person he's come to rely on most and may never see again.

http://www.dreamspinnerpress.com

ANDREW GREY grew up in western Michigan with a father who loved to tell stories and a mother who loved to read them. Since then he has lived all over the country and traveled throughout the world. He has a master's degree from the University of Wisconsin-Milwaukee and now works full time on his writing. Andrew's hobbies include collecting antiques, gardening, and leaving his dirty dishes anywhere but in the sink (particularly when writing). He considers himself blessed with an accepting family, fantastic friends, and the world's most supportive and loving husband. Andrew currently lives in beautiful historic Carlisle, Pennsylvania.

Visit Andrew's website at http://www.andrewgreybooks.com and blog at http://andrewgreybooks.livejournal.com/.
E-mail him at andrewgrey@comcast.net.

Blair Montague is sent to Newton, Montana, to purchase a ranch and some land for his father. It's a trip he doesn't want to make. But his father paid for his college education in exchange for Blair working for him in his casinos, so Blair has no choice. When he finds out he'll be dealing with Royal Masters, the man who bullied him in high school, he is shocked. Then Blair is surprised when he finds that Royal's time in the Marines has changed him to the point where Blair could be attracted to him… if he's willing to take that chance.

Royal's life hasn't been a bed of roses. He saw combat in the military that left him scarred, and not just on the outside. When he inherits his father's ranch, he discovers his father wasn't a good manager and the ranch is in trouble. The sale of land would put them back on good footing, but he is suspicious of Blair's father's motives, and with good reason. The attraction between them is hard for either to ignore, but it could all evaporate once the land deal is sealed.

http://www.dreamspinnerpress.com

On the train from Lancaster to Philadelphia, Trent runs into Brit, his first love and the first man to break his heart. They've both been through a lot in the years since they parted ways, and as they talk, the old connection tenuously strengthens. Trent finally works up the nerve to call Brit, and their rekindled friendship slowly grows into the possibility for more. But both men are shadowed by their pasts as they explore the path they didn't take the first time. If they can move beyond loss and painful memories, they might find their road leads to a second chance at happiness.

A story from the Dreamspinner Press 2015 Daily Dose package "Never Too Late."

http://www.dreamspinnerpress.com

Hunter Wolf is a highly paid Las Vegas escort with a face and body that have men salivating and paying a great deal for him to fulfill their fantasies. He keeps his own fantasies to himself, not that they matter.

Grant is an elementary-school teacher who works miracles with his summer school students. He discovered his gift while in high school, tutoring Hunter, a fellow student. They meet again when Hunter rescues Grant in a club. Grant doesn't know Hunter is an escort or that they share similarly painful pasts involving family members' substance abuse.

After the meeting, Hunter invites Grant to one of the finest restaurants in Las Vegas. Hunter is charming, sexy, and gracious, and Grant is intrigued. With more in common than they realized, the two men decide to give a relationship a try. At first, Grant believes he can deal with Hunter's profession and accepts that Hunter will be faithful with his heart if not his body. Both men find their feelings run deeper than either imagined. For Grant, it's harder than he thought to accept Hunter's occupation, and Hunter's feelings for Grant now make work nearly impossible. But Hunter's choice of profession comes with a price, which could involve Grant's job and their hearts—a price that might be too high for either of them to pay.

http://www.dreamspinnerpress.com

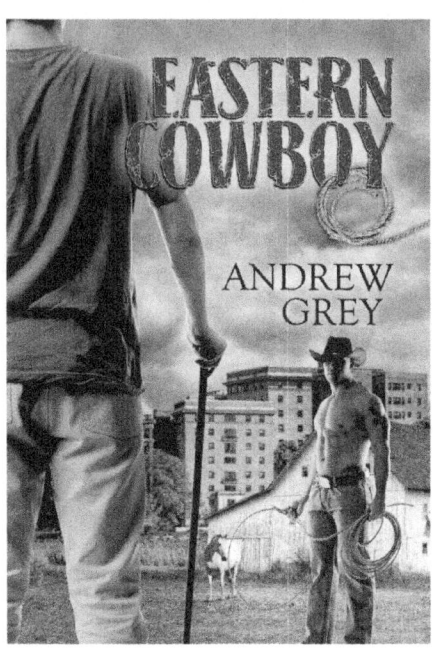

Brighton McKenzie inherited one of the last pieces of farmland in suburban Baltimore. It has been in his family since Maryland was a colony, though it has lain fallow for years. Selling it for development would be easy, but Brighton wants to honor his grandfather's wishes and work it again. Unfortunately, an accident left him relying on a cane, so he'll need help. Tanner Houghton used to work on a ranch in Montana until a vengeful ex got him fired because of his sexuality. He comes to Maryland at the invitation of his cousin and is thrilled to have a chance to get back to the kind of work he loves.

Brighton is instantly drawn to the intensely handsome and huge Tanner—he's everything Brighton likes in a man, though he holds back because Tanner is an employee, and because he can't understand why a man as virile as Tanner would be interested in him. But that isn't the worst of their problems. They have to face the machinations of Brighton's aunt, Tanner's ex suddenly wanting him back, and the need to find a way to make the farm financially viable before they lose Brighton's family legacy.

http://www.dreamspinnerpress.com

A Chaotic RANGE

ANDREW GREY

Most of the time ranchhand David rescues stray cattle, but this time he and his fellow cowboys Wally and Haven save a stranded motorist. David is surprised to find his former high school classmate nearly frozen in his car. After learning that Brian Applewright's boss fired him from his ranch for being gay, they invite him back to theirs to take a job.

David and Brian moved in different social circles at school, but working together brings them closer. However, David has a rocky history on the ranch. The foreman is his ex, and he only recently returned after a heartbreakingly unsuccessful attempt to find greener pastures. He can't risk his heart getting close to anyone.

But on a ranch, nature has a way of forcing an issue. When a snowstorm threatens, David and Brian head out to mend a fence and round up some stray cattle. David gets injured, and they must survive in the snow, cold, and wind. It might be the start of a relationship... or the end of their lives.

http://www.dreamspinnerpress.com

Duncan is an ocean from home over the holidays and expects to spend them alone. To his pleasant surprise, one of his European coworkers, Georg, befriends him and includes Duncan in the holiday traditions of his homeland: cutting a Christmas tree under starry skies at Georg's country estate, decorating it at the family's city home, and shopping at the Christmas market in Munich. Both men are lonely and realize they have much in common. But Georg's life is in Germany and Duncan's is in Boston. With the project they're working on nearing completion, any chance for more than a holiday fling seems as elusive as stardust.

http://www.dreamspinnerpress.com

Officer Red Markham knows about the ugly side of life after a car accident left him scarred and his parents dead. His job policing the streets of Carlisle, PA, only adds to the ugliness, and lately, drug overdoses have been on the rise. One afternoon, Red is dispatched to the local Y for a drowning accident involving a child. Arriving on site, he finds the boy rescued by lifeguard Terry Baumgartner. Of course, Red isn't surprised when gorgeous Terry won't give him and his ugly mug the time of day.

Overhearing one of the officers comment about him being shallow opens Terry's eyes. Maybe he isn't as kindhearted as he always thought. His friend Julie suggests he help those less fortunate by delivering food to the elderly. On his route he meets outspoken Margie, a woman who says what's on her mind. Turns out, she's Officer Red's aunt.

Red and Terry's worlds collide as Red tries to track the source of the drugs and protect Terry from an ex-boyfriend who won't take no for an answer. Together they might discover a chance for more than they expected—if they can see beyond what's on the surface.

http://www.dreamspinnerpress.com

Carter Schunk is a dedicated police officer with a difficult past and a big heart. When he's called to a domestic disturbance, he finds a fatally injured woman, and a child, Alex, who is in desperate need of care. Child Services is called, and the last man on earth Carter wants to see walks through the door. Carter had a fling with Donald a year ago and found him as cold as ice since it ended.

Donald (Ice) Ickle has had a hard life he shares with no one, and he's closed his heart to all. It's partly to keep himself from getting hurt and partly the way he deals with a job he's good at, because he does what needs to be done without getting emotionally involved. When he meets Carter again, he maintains his usual distance, but Carter gets under his skin, and against his better judgment, Donald lets Carter guilt him into taking Alex when there isn't other foster care available. Carter even offers to help care for the boy.

Donald has a past he doesn't want to discuss with anyone, least of all Carter, who has his own past he'd just as soon keep to himself. But it's Alex's secrets that could either pull them together or rip them apart—secrets the boy isn't able to tell them and yet could be the key to happiness for all of them.

http://www.dreamspinnerpress.com

Kendall Monroe is handcuffed to a car in the desert.

Is this life imitating art or art imitating life? The only thing he's sure of is that the situation he finds himself in is a copy of a scene he filmed earlier, only this time, there is no director yelling "cut" and no crew to rescue him. Terrified for his life, Kendall takes comfort remembering happier times with his longtime lover, Johnny. He hasn't seen Johnny in weeks since Johnny stayed behind to finish his latest best-selling novel.

As he attempts to survive scorching-hot days and freezing nights, Kendall tries to figure out who did this to him. Could it be Johnny, or the research assistant he suspects Johnny is having an affair with? Both options fill him with bitterness. Or is it a more likely suspect? Kendall has a stalker who sends him flowers and always seems to know where he is. But what does this stranger have to gain by leaving Kendall stranded in the middle of nowhere?

http://www.dreamspinnerpress.com

On the day he and Roman Capanelli were to be married, Malik Stevens wakes up in a small room with very little light. Time must be passing, because a door opens from time to time and food is left for him—that's his only connection to the outside world. Roman is a choreographer on Broadway, and he's waiting for Malik at the park with all their friends, ready to start their marriage ceremony. When Malik doesn't show up, Roman is nearly heartbroken thinking he's been left at the altar. But soon he understands that Malik hasn't stood him up, he's been taken.

Desperate and determined, Roman begins searching for clues to aid the police. Then, when Malik escapes, the couple continues the search until they ferret out the culprit, and in the process open up a box of secrets. An orphan who grew up in a foster home, Malik knows his father was a serial killer and his mother died of grief and shame after his father was convicted. Now it seems some of his parents' skeletons still hang in the family closet. But was Malik's kidnapping meant to uncover those secrets or to hide them forever?

http://www.dreamspinnerpress.com

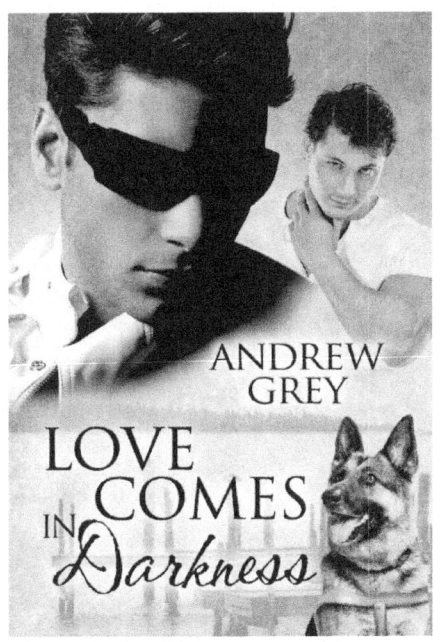

Howard Justinian has always had to fight for his freedom. Because he was born blind, everyone is always trying to shelter him, but he's determined to live his life on his own terms.

When an argument with his boyfriend over that hard-won self-reliance leaves Howard stranded by the side of the road, assistance arrives in the form of Gordy Jarrett. Gordy is a missionary's son, so helping others is second nature—and he does it in such an unassuming manner that Howard can't say no.

Life is barely back on track when Howard receives shocking news: his sister died, leaving him her daughter to care for. Howard now faces his greatest challenge yet: for Sophia's safety, he'll need to accept help, but will he learn to accept it from Gordy, the one man who will not curb his independence?

http://www.dreamspinnerpress.com

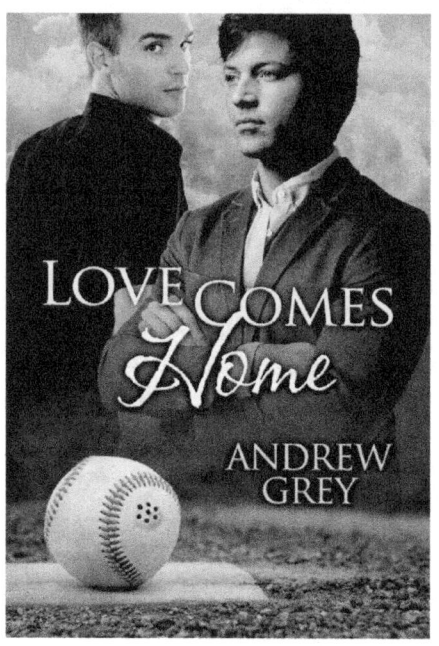

When architect Gregory Hampton's son, Davey, starts having trouble in Little League, Greg takes him to an eye doctor. The diagnosis hits them hard. Davey's sight is degenerating rapidly, and eventually he'll go blind.

Tom Spangler is used to getting what he wants. When Greg captures his attention, he asks Greg for a date. They have a good time until Greg gets a call from the friends watching his son, telling him Davey has fallen. Greg and Tom return to find the worst has happened—Davey can no longer see.

With so much going on in his life, Greg doubts he'll see Tom again. But Tom has researched beep baseball, where balls and bases make sounds to enable the visually impaired to participate in Little League. Tom spearheads an effort to form a team so Davey can continue to play the game he loves. But when Greg's ex-wife shows up with her doctor boyfriend, offering a possible cure through a radical procedure, Greg must decide how far he'll go to give Davey a chance at getting his sight back.

http://www.dreamspinnerpress.com

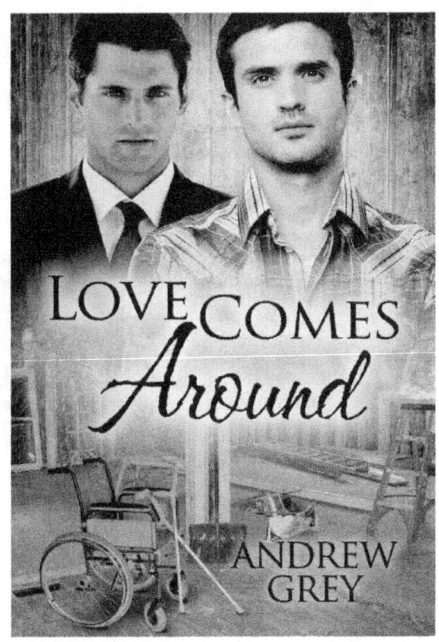

Dan was a throwaway child and learned to take care of himself in foster care. As an adult, he devotes his life to the business he started and his heart to raising children no one else wants. Dan has already adopted six-year-old Lila, who walks on crutches, and then decides to adopt eight-year-old Jerry, who suffers from MD and is confined to a wheelchair.

Also abandoned as a child, Connor ended up on his own and retreated into himself. He works as a carpenter and woodcarver and is the perfect man to ensure Dan's home becomes wheelchair accessible.

When Dan hires Connor, neither of the men are ready to open their hearts to the possibility of love. As they learn how much they have in common, both of them must weigh the possibility of family and a future against the risks of getting hurt again.

http://www.dreamspinnerpress.com

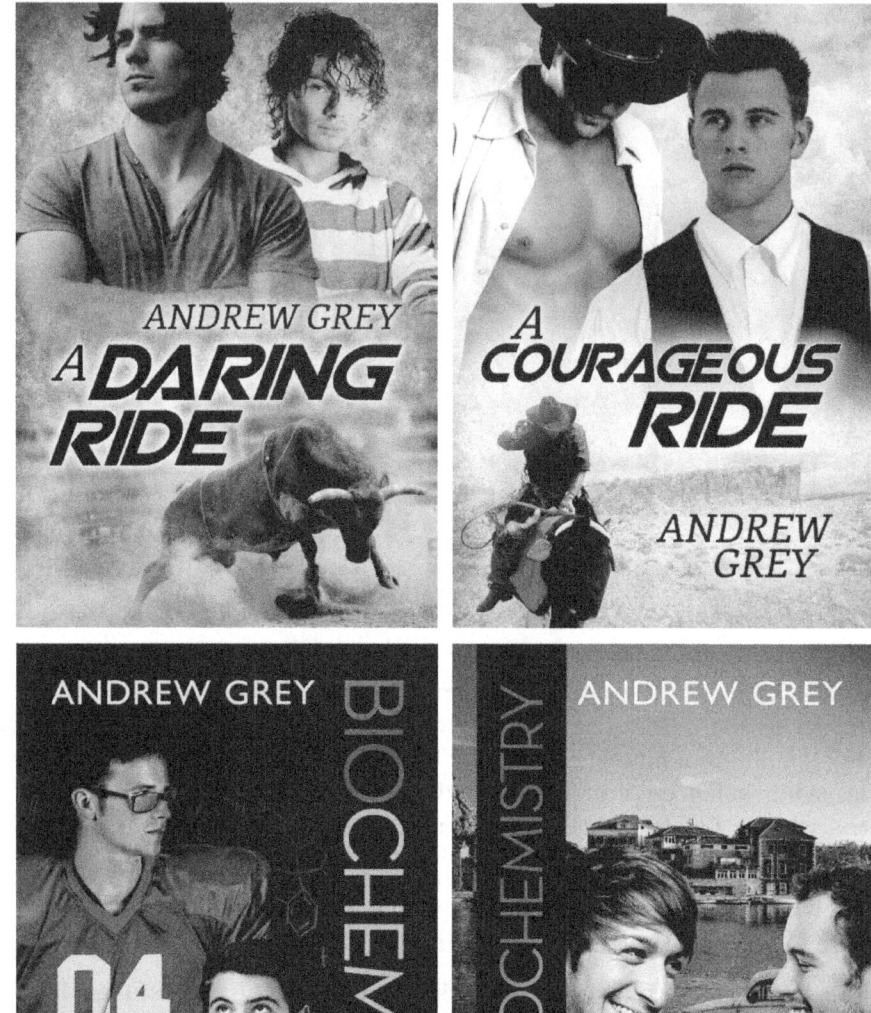

http://www.dreamspinnerpress.com

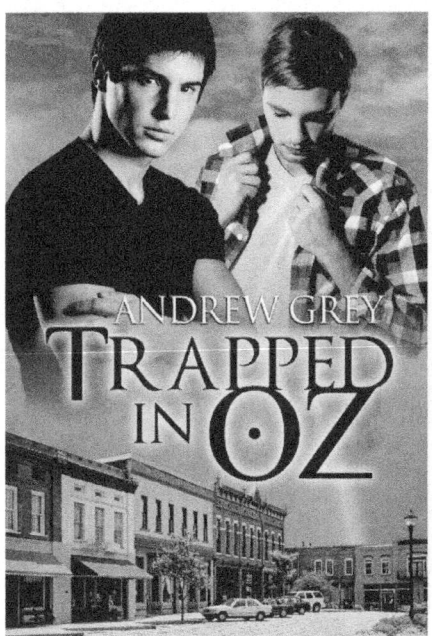

http://www.dreamspinnerpress.com

INSIDE OUT

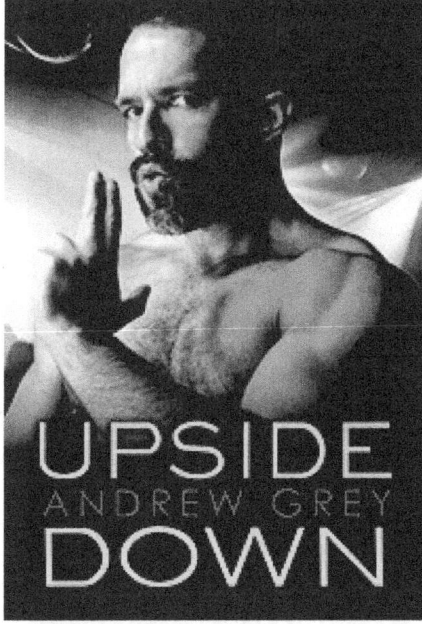

UPSIDE
ANDREW GREY
DOWN

BACKWARD
ANDREW GREY

http://www.dreamspinnerpress.com

Made in the USA
Las Vegas, NV
19 October 2024